WANDLESS

James Batchelor

Cover by Parry-Hide Photography
www.parryhidephotography.co.uk

Fonts: Berylium by Typodermic Fonts,
Portland LDO by Luke Owens

For regular updates on future books, including more Wandless stories,
please subscribe to my mailing list

subscribe.jamesbatchelor.me

To Grandad
For his encouragement and support

I reckon they have bookshops in Heaven

1

Keep running. No matter what she heard behind her, she had to keep running. It was the only way to fend off the paralysis of fear.

Emilia knew her footsteps were too loud. They pounded the earth, announcing her to the darkness, accompanied by the occasional loud rustle of bushes and shrubs as she barged past them. The leaves whispered loudly, cheerleaders to her escape. But no time to slow down and silence them. She had to keep running.

The cold night air chilled her lungs. It was refreshing at first, but she knew it wouldn't be long before it started to burn. She needed to be far away by then, far enough to find somewhere to hide and catch her breath. Emilia had never been particularly active before she was sent to the Sanctuary, and there had been no incentive or facilities to improve on that, but she was determined to push beyond her limits tonight. She had no choice. There was nothing more motivating than death.

Her eyes focused on the darkness ahead, picking out vague shapes of bushes and trees, but her ears strained to hear what was behind her. Between the thumping of her footsteps, distressed voices called to each other. She couldn't make out the words, but knew what they were saying. She's escaped. Stop her.

A dark wall loomed ahead, but the inconsistency of its blackness told her it was the tree line, not something solid. For so long she had peered at these trees through the fence, an almost daily ritual of wishful thinking. They had seemed so far, but she was already close enough to touch them.

No time to savour the moment. Push through them and keep running. A sharp scrape along her shoulder showed the trees' disdain for her, offended by the lack of reverence. The pain lingered, a welcome distraction from the early indicators of fatigue. If they had fed her properly, if she was well-rested, this sprint wouldn't affect her so badly - but that was the point, wasn't it?

Something soft, damp and loud came up to her waist as she thrashed through it. Emilia reached out to the sides and felt long stalks; some sort of crop, possibly wheat. Didn't matter what type, it was going to get her killed.

Bright lights punctured the darkness, scattered into angular beams by the trees behind her and she could hear the the growl of the quad bikes. It would be seconds before they pierced through this field and their headlights found her. Even if she hid, the trail she carved through the wheat would betray her.

Despair threatened to grip her, force her to accept her fate, but there was something different about the air on this side of the trees. Maybe it was her imagination but it tasted fresher, less icy than when she began her escape. There was a hint of warmth as well, but it wasn't oppressive. In fact, everything felt lighter, her head clearer. A numbing ache she hadn't realised was there had lifted, although the throbbing of her heartbeat remained.

Then she understood. The suppression field.

With every frantic step she took, every incremental increase in the distance between herself and the Sanctuary, Emilia felt stronger. Her pulse transformed from desperation to determination, pumping with a forgotten power. The corners of her mouth twitched into a grin.

The roar of the bikes killed any seeds of optimism. She was still outnumbered, outpaced, outgunned and out of options. One passed dangerously close to her and she was shocked she wasn't spotted. The noise of the bikes must be drowning out the rustling wheat, the drivers focused only on what they could see in the path of their headlights.

Then, the inevitable. Another bike came up far behind her, headlights bathing her in treacherous radiance. Something in her wanted to stop, to give up, but it was quickly overruled by the invigoration that grew as she moved further and further from the suppression field. Keep running.

Wheat disintegrated around her before her brain processed the sounds of gunfire. Adrenaline afforded her another gear and she briefly picked up speed, barrelling towards the next tree line on the other side of the field. Five more steps and she'd be there. The trees rustled in pain as bullets ripped through them, more thudding into the bark as she passed.

Instinctively, Emilia reached out for a tree trunk to halt herself, ducking from sight. The trees were close together here, so the quad bikes would be forced further down the field's edge to wider gaps. Sure enough, they rumbled away and Emilia was plunged into darkness again. She watched with a mix of fear and defiance as they swerved into the next wheat field and swung around.

There was no way to get past them. More would be on the way soon, if they weren't already. The bullet shells scattered through the devastated wheat behind her showed there was no interest in taking her back to the Sanctuary alive. She hugged the tree, but somehow managed to hold back hopeless tears. No, it wasn't self-restraint controlling those tears - it was the rising strength that had been growing with every step.

The fight-or-flight instinct that had been tearing her apart since first crossing the fence suddenly took a violent swing towards the former. No longer was she despairing, she was determined. Not fearful, but furious. And far more powerful than they realised.

It had been years since Emilia had used her magic but muscle memory kicked in and she quickly felt that familiar warm glow from the pit of her stomach. Reaching deep within herself, she focused on that feeling and fuelled it, until it filled her chest, her shoulders and spilled into her arms. Every inch of her skin tensed, until she was unsure whether she was being suffocated by her own body or trying to burst out of her fleshy prison. She had forgotten this exquisite cocktail of pain and pleasure.

The quad bikes were advancing, nearly back to the treeline, their searchlights scanning the length of the field. Still hiding behind a thick trunk, Emilia could feel them out there. Four of them - three men, one woman - in a perfect horizontal line. It was too dark to see them as anything more than menacing silhouettes, yet in her mind she could picture every detail. Another force fuelled her power of perception, one she now remembered how to channel. Some of her companions back at the Sanctuary were once able to perceive emotions and even unspoken thoughts, but that gift still eluded her. Even without it, she could sense how determined they were to find her.

She stepped out from behind the tree into the light, blinded but only in terms of her optical sight.

"She's there," one of the men called. "The Carrier."

"What the hell are you waiting for?" the woman replied, evidently the leader.

Their words were muffled as Emilia concentrated. Without a wand to channel her power, she was forced to use her hands, stretching out to direct the magic through tense fingers. She hadn't done this since she first started developing her gift as a teenager - as soon as anyone showed signs of magical abilities, they were issued with a wand to keep it under control, to direct it more accurately. At least, that used to be the case.

Her hands shook as she struggled to restrain the power, to focus it. Part of her wanted to fully unleash just to see what happened, but horror stories of untamed magic ripping its user apart held her back. That had been another reason wands were issued: for the user's safety.

The key, she remembered, was to concentrate on a specific task - or, in her case, specific objects. Over the aggressive growl of the quad bikes, she could just about hear the pathetic click of a mechanical failure.

"My gun's jammed," the driver on the far right shouted.

"Mine too."

"It's her," the woman scowled. "She's too far from the suppression field."

"What do we - whoa!"

The two end drivers cried out in unison as their bikes began to lift into the air and towards each other. All four of them shouted over each other, but Emilia tuned this cacophany out and concentrated on lifting the other two. Her power hadn't put her body under this much pressure since long before she was captured. Locking four rifles and moving four quad bikes was tough, even before years without magic. The bikes were heavy, more in mental effort than physical weight. But every inch she managed to move them gave her fresh strength. Emilia's face bunched up tightly, no need to visibly see her enemies while their pulsing forms took shape in her mind.

She found new reserves within herself and sped up the bikes' flight. Over the throbbing in her ears, the pulsing ache at the front of her skull, the drivers screamed in panic as they hurtled upwards. She had expected them to jump clear of their vehicles, but they clung on until it was too late to do so.

With a twist of her outstretched hands, the four bikes flipped over and she released them. The sudden relief threatened to make her collapse, but she stood firm. The fall sent the soldiers' screams up several octaves, but only for a second. A crunch of metal and bone marked the impact of each quad bike, a short and awful rhythm that echoed through the night air.

Silence.

Emilia didn't know if the drivers were unconscious or dead, nor could she process her feelings if they were the latter. There was no time to celebrate or feel relief. The Sanctuary was still close enough to have heard the crash, which means more soldiers would be on the way. Not that she couldn't handle them now.

Emilia kept running.

2

There was minimal security protecting the nearby villages and towns when compared to the Sanctuary. Clearly, the government never believed a Wandless could get far enough away from the suppression field to warrant installing more troops in the area.

Evading the second wave of quad bikes became much easier for Emilia after reclaiming her magic. Through her unique ability, she could sense the drivers - as if they, too, had powers that were calling out to her. Paranoia, surely, although it did make her wonder why the government had never recruited witches and wizards to keep other magic users in check - unlike the Americans, who recruited them into the military. Most likely the politicians didn't trust any Wandless. After all, that's what led to places like the Sanctuary and the invention of the suppression field.

Despite the military's presence diminishing as she travelled further than the Sanctuary, Emilia had some soul-chilling close encounters. At one point, another line of quads rode right past her, but she managed to roll under a fallen tree before they noticed. They slowed to a crawl, powerful torches sweeping the dark landscape.

She lay in the damp grass beneath the toppled tree for at least twenty minutes before an opportunity to move forward arose, most of which she spent wishing she'd been one of those witches that had learned how to influence other people's thoughts. That was perhaps the biggest disadvantage of being Wandless; without a wand to harness their power, magic users were limited to their natural ability, most often specialised in a single area. Even with a wand, few ever mastered multiple forms of magic.

Eventually, the bikes dispersed, snarling off towards the nearest town. That should have been enough reason not to continue in the same direction, but without knowing the surrounding area it would be beyond foolish to attempt a cross-country hike, much as she had enjoyed those in the past. Emilia wouldn't have known where to travel, where she might find food or shelter or transport, or even who she might encounter. Darkness disorientates and she couldn't risk stumbling upon another Sanctuary - or somehow ending up back at her own.

As she approached the town, crouched down and waddling along the bed of a wide stream, she could see the bikes again. Three seemed to be circling the outskirts, and judging from the sounds and moving lights from between the buildings, the other two must have been patrolling every street. Her pursuers were blemishes on what would otherwise have been a picturesque moonlit scene. Under other circumstances, this would have made a great addition to her sketchbook.

Even without actively tapping into her power, Emilia could just about feel each driver and bike in her mind. Prior to her capture, she was accustomed to this background connection to whatever was around her, with a particular emphasis on whatever or whoever she focused on. For Emilia, this was the norm and she had been confused when she learned not everyone viewed the world the way she did.

She froze as the first of the three patrolling bikes appeared in the distance to her left, rolling past a quaint, traditional pub as it came into view. She crouched even lower, briefly struggling to maintain her balance and avoid falling over into the shallow but icy water. Reeds obscured her from view, but she dared not look up to see whether the bikes had passed. Even in the darkness, movement attracts attention. Time slowed, the growling of the bikes became more aggressive as they got closer, but Emilia stayed perfectly still, scarcely daring to breathe. Even if she had no magical power, she wouldn't have needed to look up to know when they passed; the sound of their engines faded as they continued their vigil around the town and eventually rolled out of sight.

There was no knowing how long it would take them to circle the entire town, but Emilia couldn't afford to waste much more time. The fact that the soldiers came here meant they expected her, knowing there was nowhere else to go for miles.

She glanced up to check the way was clear, climbed out of the stream bed and ran. Her mind and magic constantly monitored the movements of the five bikes, but her eyes remained rigidly focused on the pub ahead, feet pounding on the grass. For a chilling second, she thought she saw headlights beaming in her direction, but as she risked a glance to her right, she saw it was only an upstairs light turning on in one of the nearest houses.

The pub was getting closer now, but so were the three patrolling bikes as they rounded the cruelly small town. Emilia released the pub from a determined gaze and searched for a hiding place. There were none. Her options shrank dramatically: either she reached her destination before the soldiers spotted her, or she had to confront all three. There was no doubt she would survive such a skirmish but the other two bikes would be alerted, and this close to the town there would be witnesses, making it harder to flee the area undetected. It would also present the danger of damaging property or harming innocents, which was what had vilified witchkind in the first place.

Emilia kept running. Her feet ached from the ongoing escape, so much more than they did back in the fields near the Sanctuary. There was a sharp jolt of pain as the ground beneath her switched from grass to tarmac, combined with a surge of relief: it was the road, which meant five more steps until she reached the pub's parking area. Emilia ducked behind a rusting farmer's truck just as the three bikes passed by, and she risked standing up to watch as they stalked away into the night.

Given how quickly they completed their last circuit, she couldn't risk hastily stealing a vehicle now - they would see her on the road as they circled the town again. Instead, she weighed up her options - limited though they were - so she would be ready to move the second they passed again.

The sudden change of pace exacerbated her exhaustion. Aching feet were accompanied by stinging lungs, a pounding headache and shooting pains spreading across her body that fought to stop her from concentrating. All were signs of fatigue from her flight and... the other thing. But the distant sound of the quad bikes' growling, the nagging connection between her mind and the searching drivers, gave her no time to rest.

Emilia stepped out from behind the truck and surveyed the other vehicles parked outside the pub. There wasn't much variety: a couple of larger vehicles similar to the truck, two people carriers and a single compact car. Nothing sleek or quick - clearly the patrons of this pub weren't exactly wealthy.

She crept over to the compact car and placed a hand

over the lock on the driver's door. Focusing her power, she temporarily released the connection to the soldiers and concentrated on the mechanism. Magically jamming the guns had been less intensive - since handheld objects tend to be simpler, she merely had to compress or strain all the parts she could reach with her mind. This, however, was a larger, clunkier mechanism and, worse still, one connected to a car alarm. Without a wand, even a tactile connection to the object she wished to manipulate would be imprecise.

Emilia closed her eyes to better visualise what was happening within the door, almost allowing her to see inside the lock, to move individual parts and see how they interacted with others. She did so cautiously. Without a wand to focus her power, she could inadvertently move multiple pieces at once. By the time she figured out how to unlock it, Emilia could hear the distant hum of the quad bikes again.

With a frighteningly loud click, perhaps amplified by the previously tense silence, the door opened and she climbed inside, pulling it carefully shut behind her. Even though she knew they wouldn't be able to see her from their patrol route, the car obscured by the corner of the building, she huddled down in the driver's seat until they were gone. As the sound of the bikes began to fade again, she sat up and placed her hands on the wheel, mentally feeling her way to the ignition. This was simpler than the door lock, with less fear of tripping an alarm, and the car roared into life. Emilia's eyes widened and her head snapped to the right, but the last quad was just disappearing around the corner of the furthest house.

Hoping the engine noise wouldn't wake anyone sleeping in the pub above her, or attract the attention of late night drinkers behind the wall next to her, she reversed without looking - there was no need for wing mirrors when you had a latent magical awareness of all large objects and structures around you. She stalled briefly as she pulled forward, trying not to think about how many years it had been since she had driven any kind of vehicle, but a sharp jolt with her power and the engine kicked in again. She eased the car out onto the country lane and turned away from the town.

Keeping the headlights off, there was nothing but darkness ahead and the shrinking lights of both the town and the quad bikes behind her.

3

Captain Amanda Hawthorne sat in the back of the sleek black car and glared at the TV built into the driver's headrest. The driver himself remained silent, just as Hawthorne preferred. Cars and lorries fell behind them as they sped up the motorway, the scenery slipping past too fast to focus on, but the Captain ignored all this for the news, sound transmitted wirelessly to the headphones previously tucked into the door compartment.

Flashy graphics indicated the beginning of a fresh segment on this channel, before sliding away to reveal a smiling host and three panelists. Hawthorne already knew what the topic of discussion would be. It could be nothing else.

"Good morning, you're watching Daily Debrief and I'm Anne Scuttlethorpe," said the brunette now filling the screen, her enthusiasm as fake as her wrinkle-free cheeks. "As you heard before the break, a Wandless Carrier - one Miss Emilia Harris - broke out of her assigned Sanctuary near Little Finchingford last night and has eluded all efforts to recapture her. The woman has already killed four of the Anti-Magic Security Force personnel dispatched to apprehend her and civilians across Yorkshire are being advised to stay at home, travelling only when necessary while further troops are deployed to the area. Anyone travelling will be asked to show their identification and potentially be held briefly for questioning. The AMSF is calling for full co-operation in this matter."

A photo of a middle-aged woman appeared on the floor-to-ceiling screen behind Scuttlethorpe. Hawthorne studied the face, even though it was smaller and less clear than the one in the dossier on the seat beside her. The smile seemed pleasant, the eyes joyful, but the Captain knew it was a facade. Behind this humble face was a superiority, the knowledge that she could do something normal people could never - and should never - hope to do. Hawthorne had seen it before.

Scuttlethorpe was still talking, staring into the depths of the camera as if expecting it to smile back.

"In the meantime, we have former AMSF Sergeant John Wilkington, Greater Oxford University's Professor of Witchkind Studies Dr Phoebe Harrington-Jones, and founder of the protest group Free The Wandless, Robert Quinn. Thank you all for joining me today.

"Mr Wilkington, I'd like to turn to you first. How has the AMSF allowed this to happen? The magical population has been largely under control for almost a decade and while there have been a few incidents of escape, they have always been resolved within hours. Are security standards lapsing? What should the AMSF be doing to assure the public that this is an isolated incident?"

The taller man straightened in his seat, as if to make himself look more impressive. To Hawthorne, it was a fruitless attempt; he used to look more intimidating in the uniform, the one she now wore. She wished she'd had the chance to work with him but the General had robbed her of that. His dismissal had been a face-saving exercise for the AMSF but Hawthorne knew that escaping Wandless had deserved the death Wilkington delivered.

"Well, Anne," Wilkington said, "for a start I want to make it clear that I'm not going to bad-mouth or criticise the work done by my former colleagues. While we know a great deal about the Wandless threat, these men and women are still risking everything to contain an unprecedented force and they're doing a remarkably good job given the circumstances. The Sanctuary system is perhaps the most advanced infrastructure of its kind and it's absolutely the best solution that this country, or any other, has come up with for keeping the magic population docile. I used to work in one of these Sanctuaries as you well know, and both the AMSF troops and the witchkind residents focus all their efforts on keeping the peace. It works out best for both sides."

Scuttlethorpe frowned, as much as her face would let her. "Yes, but a resident has now escaped and she's taken lives while doing so. It's understandable that the public, the human viewers of this show, might be more than a little concerned. Is that peace making the AMSF complacent? Has this set a precedent that will encourage further uprisings at the other Sanctuaries?"

Hawthorne bristled and bit her lip. Scuttlethorpe was lucky Wilkington was on the panel instead of her. In her mind, a response formed but her former peer voiced it for her.

"Let's get a little perspective, Anne," he said in the commanding voice of an ex-soldier. "This is not an uprising, this is a single escape involving only one Wandless. Nothing like the Sanctuary system has even been tried before, so there will inevitably be the occasional teething problem. You yourself just said all previous escapes have been handled within hours, but it was inevitable a witch or wizard might one day surpass this.

The AMSF troops are the finest I've ever served with and I'll guarantee she'll be back at her Sanctuary by the end of the day."

Hawthorne allowed herself a subtle smile and checked her watch. They were still not due at their destination for half an hour or so. Most of the journey had been spent reading the dossier, but the pertinent information simply reiterated everything she had been told at the briefing a few hours ago. After the third reading, she had turned to the news, a brief distraction to kill time while she travelled and a source of amusement as she gauged how little the media and public knew.

The other man on the panel spoke, the smaller one in the plain polo shirt bearing the cheaply embroidered FTW logo. "I'm sorry but can I just interrupt, Mrs Scuttlethorpe? We need to stop calling them 'Sanctuaries' and use a more correct term: concentration camps."

Hawthorne's jaw clenched. Of all the ignorant...

"Mr Quinn, please - " Scuttlethorpe said, but the fool continued.

"I'm serious. The AMSF may not be torturing those poor Wandless like the military used to do a century ago, but the concept is the same - a specific group from within the population, our population, confined to a high-security location and cut off from the rest of the world. It's a punishment, a punishment simply for being who they are."

Wilkington swung round in his chair and looked down on the man.

"Now wait a minute, sir, I don't know if you've ever been to one of the Sanctuaries but I was stationed at one in Devon for years and your comments are way off the mark. Every witch or wizard there was happy, comfortable, they had their own homes - not cells, homes. Let's not forget every Sanctuary used to be a country village, generously donated by the residents to help the effort in rehabilitating witchkind. And, I say again, those Wandless are happy. They come to no harm..."

Quinn did a remarkable job on hiding any signs of intimidation. "The suppression field, Mr Wilkington. The suppression field is doing them harm, by preventing them from using their natural abilities..."

"There is nothing natural about their abilities - "

"... and while I may not have personally been to these camps, we have several members at FTW who were former guards like yourself. They have told us about how the Wandless are mistreated, forced to work menial jobs that even human prisoners aren't subjected to. They are robbed of their privacy, unable to even call or e-mail their families without supervision or someone monitoring and approving their message."

Wilkington's face was awash with frustration and despair. "For safety, Mr Quinn, both ours and theirs. The whole point of the Sanctuary system and the stringent security measures put in place is for everyone's safety. In the nine years since the first Sanctuary opened, there has not been a single magic-caused death, let alone anything on the scale of the Harwich Massacre. The system is working."

The reference to Harwich made Hawthorne tense. Flashes of that day fought their way to the forefront of her mind, faces in the crowds staring at her with either narrowed determination or wide-eyed horror. Harris was among the latter, but that made her no less disturbing. The captain had spent the past decade ensuring everyone involved in that atrocity was contained, and she was not about to let one slip the net. She brushed the memories aside and considered turning the television off before Quinn could respond, but curiosity got the better of her.

"What about Wandless deaths? What about the AMSF and...?"

Scuttlethorpe spoke over them. "Gentlemen, I'm sorry, I'm going to have to interrupt as we only have a limited time this morning. I'm going to bring in Dr Harrington-Jones to the discussion now: Doctor, what is the Wandless capable of now she's no longer contained by the suppression field?"

The woman, who had been watching the two men quietly as if observing animals in the wild, straightened her blouse and sat forward.

"So, this woman is going to be going through a lot of mental and physical trauma," she began. "I'm not familiar with her specific powers, but they have been suppressed for so long, her body under invisible pressure for a number of years now. That puts a remarkable amount of strain on someone, even as strong as her. She'll need time to get to grips with her powers again. It's like if she were blind for any amount of time, and then she regains her sight: there's an adjustment period for the brain to get used to processing that sort of sensory information again.

"Whether or not she can handle that is another matter. Unfortunately, there just hasn't been enough research into how Homo Magus react to the return of their powers - quite frankly, most of the research that went into developing the suppression field focused on quite the opposite. It could be that she needs to re-learn how to control her abilities again, and there's no telling how long that will take. Let's also not forget that the reason they had wands in the first place was to channel that magic, to better harness it. Without her wand, her powers will be more unwieldy."

"Does that make her more dangerous than the AMSF has already stated, Doctor?" Scuttlethorpe asked, flashing a warning look at Quinn before he could interrupt.

"Quite possibly," Harrington-Jones said. "The tragic deaths of those soldiers last night may not have been intentional. The Wandless may have been trying to incapacitate them, perhaps distract or confuse them - we know from before the Sanctuaries were established that some of these people had the ability to manipulate minds. It might be that she is unable to control herself and is unintentionally lethal. This, in turn, might be amplified by the fact she's a Carrier. There have been no opportunities to study a Wandless in her situation, so there are a lot of unknowns. As such, she must be approached with extreme caution - even by the most highly trained AMSF forces."

Quinn slammed his hands down on the arms of his chair. "I'm sorry, but can we also stop using this term 'Carrier'?"

"Mr Quinn, I..."

"No, it's unnecessary military slang that's been used to create fear over something perfectly normal, part of the vilification of witchkind - beyond their special and unique abilities, they're no different to us. They're people. So let's stop saying she's a Carrier. Let's call a spade a spade, and say she's..."

Scuttlethorpe held a hand up, and the camera cut away from the wide shot of the panel, focusing solely on the host.

"Mr Quinn, I really must stop you there as we've run out of time. We're now going live to an interview with the Overseer of the Little Finchingford Sanctuary with advice for civilians on how to resist magical manipulation until the escaped Wandless has been apprehended. We'll be back with more Daily Debrief this afternoon - until then, I'm Anne Scuttlethope."

The camera zoomed out and more graphics came in to

obscure Scuttlethorpe and the panelists, while a voiceover informed viewers what was coming up. Hawthorne reached forward for the buttons beneath the screen and turned it off.

Quinn's pathetic voice echoed in her ears. They weren't new arguments - she had heard Quinn make them for years via whichever media was foolish enough to give him a platform - but still they rankled the AMSF captain. Perhaps it was the peril of assumed knowledge; since she had a thorough understanding of the threat the Wandless possessed, she assumed that everyone she protected did. Sympathy for witchkind had been growing in recent years, and this had worried Hawthorne, but perhaps Harris' escape would remind people about the dangers within England's own society. Four AMSF deaths were tragic, and Hawthorne had already promised herself to look up and offer condolences to their families. It was up to her to stop Harris before she took any more lives.

"How long, driver?" she asked.

"Next junction, captain."

4

Hundreds of miles away, Emilia turned away from another wall-mounted TV as Scuttlethorpe finished speaking and stared down at her cup of coffee. She took a sip and once again thanked whatever higher power there may be - if any - that the driver of the car she stole left some money in one of the door compartments. There wasn't much; just enough for this much-needed caffeine boost and a pastry. After this meagre breakfast, she would be penniless again.

By dawn, she had travelled dozens of miles, all in as straight a direction as country roads would allow. Signposts regularly encouraged her to seek larger, faster roads, but she ignored them for fear of running into checkpoints or AMSF patrols. The signs also gave her hints as to where she might be, naming nearby towns and villages, but her knowledge of local geography became less than comprehensive as she passed into Northumberland.

Emilia had headed north, or as best she could, towards the Democratic Republic of Scotland. Folks in the DRS had been more compassionate in dealing with 'the magic threat', as Wilkington had put it. She had stopped driving once the signs announced she was just one mile away from the border town of Tweedmouth. Despite the peaceful relationship between Great England and the DRS, this was the only official border crossing for at least a hundred miles and, while Emilia knew how tight security would be here, if there was the slightest chance of safe passage, it would be better than finding a section of the river to swim across. The Tweed wasn't the world's widest river, but at this time of year Emilia would run the risk of pneumonia.

A mile outside Tweedmouth, she had swerved off into a field and parked the car out of sight of the road. A quick search of the car revealed a large overcoat in the boot, which she used to cover the clothes the AMSF no doubt had a description for. Then she walked. She walked and walked, pushing herself through sore feet and protesting muscles, until she had finally reached this café in the centre of town.

Only the waitress had shifted her gaze as she entered the room, but didn't react beyond a polite but unenthusiastic smile. At that time of morning, the café was mostly empty, aside from a few people coming off night shifts and a trio of older gentlemen who were so familiar with the young waitress they must be regulars. Emilia sidled down the aisle between the tables, aiming for the small booth in the far corner and sat facing the large windows that spanned one side of the café.

The distraction of coffee, pastry and the news discussion was a welcome escape from her current predicament. She was named so rarely in the segment, she could almost pretend they were talking about someone else, another desperate fugitive unsure of what to do next. But as Scuttlethorpe cut the panel short, Emilia's attention was yanked back into the room.

The café was much busier now, almost every table filled with hungry, noisy people. Not a single one faced her, but she couldn't shake the fear that all heads would snap in her direction at a moment's notice. Her face returned to the screens, albeit a younger, less disheveled face in a photo that was several years old. Before the Sanctuary, in a forgotten era of happiness and life.

Relief washed over her as she realised she was the only patron watching it. Everyone else was caught up in conversation, assuming all was well with the world unless a friend posted otherwise on their LifeStream.

Emilia glanced at her reflection in the mirror that ran along the wall next to her, a long-standing trick to make smaller establishments feel larger. When she had arrived, it was the first encounter with her reflection since the previous day, but everything from the past night had made an impact. Her skin was paler than that of the fugitive seen on the news, hair slightly greasier and with early strands of grey. The lips were duller, the eyes more desperate. It was a face devoid of hope and naivety, the qualities replaced with a waning determination. Ashamed of her new face, Emilia turned away, only to see her old one once again on the television. That face was lost forever.

She couldn't risk staying here much longer. Eventually someone would recognise her. She turned as casually as she could to face out the windows, taking in as much of the scene as possible.

Just as when she had first arrived, cars snaked around the roundabout, each driver glaring at the vehicle ahead impatiently. The line veered off down the widest road towards a tall gate, beyond which she could see the pillars of a suspension bridge. In front of the gate were clusters of jeeps and motorbikes. Black shapes milled around as the uniformed soldiers weaved between the cars - the local army regiment, cooperating with the AMSF in the search. Every now and then, passage was granted, the gates opened and the queue crawled forward.

The café was slightly too far to judge just how many guards were stationed here - almost certainly more than usual - but it had confirmed what Emilia had suspected. No, feared. There was no way for her to cross the river here. Again, she debated finding another area of town to scope out whether she could swim across, but the Tweed was at its widest here and the occasional snarl of a passing motorbike showed the army was still patrolling the area. She was lucky she hadn't been spotted on the way to the café.

Time to make her exit. There were too many people for her to use the fire exit into the alleyway behind, as she'd first planned. The only way out was the front door. Willing herself to stand, Emilia's eyes locked onto the door and the street beyond. As if aware of the danger, her magic automatically tuned to every person in the room, instinct trying to give her any advantage it could. She began to walk.

The door seemed impossibly far away, but in the corner of both her physical eye and magical sense, she saw that no one had looked in her direction. Allowing herself a brief sigh of relief, Emilia pressed on, now halfway across the room.

There was a sudden movement from the side. Someone advanced towards her from behind, from near the booth where she ate, and a voice cried out.

"Miss?"

A soft voice, high-pitched but gentle. The waitress. Emilia turned casually, cautiously. The girl's hand was outstretched, offering something she couldn't quite focus on.

"Your change, Miss."

Emilia half smiled, half laughed in relief, and waved at her dismissively.

"Keep it."

The waitress nodded, pocketing the coins. No one had watched their brief exchange, so Emilia turned back towards the front door and confidently strolled out into the crisp Northumberland air.

Immediately turning right, away from the border crossing, she rounded the first corner and marched down a quieter street. An icy surge of fear raced up her back as a motorbike emerged from another side road, but the rider sped towards the main road and the border crossing before he even glanced Emilia's way.

No other military vehicles passed her in the ten minutes it took to reach the edge of town, and she began the long walk back to where she had concealed the car. Hopefully there was still enough petrol to travel cross country and get her closer to an unguarded part of the border. Or better yet, across it.

5

Hawthorne looked down at the doctor. The woman stared defiantly back up at her, slouched slightly in her chair, legs outstretched, arms folded.

"You don't seem to be taking this too seriously, Doctor," the captain sneered, straightening up to ensure she towered over the medical professional.

"Oh, I'm very aware how serious it is, Captain," she replied. "But, frankly, I've done my part and now it's up to you and your troops."

"Done your part? In what way have you done your part? If you had, as you say, done your part, the witch would pose less of a threat and wouldn't have escaped in the first place."

The doctor scoffed and made a show of rolling her eyes. "Nonsense. If your men weren't so incompetent..."

"My men are more than competent, Doctor," the captain snapped. "They're some of the best the AMSF have to offer. And yet four of them are dead now, thanks to the Wandless you let get away. When the Overseer hears this..."

The doctor stood, the sudden force of movement causing her chair to wheel back. "No, don't try to pull that crap. You're not pinning this on me. I did everything by the book."

"Then why was the operation not carried out?"

The doctor's eyes rolled upwards and she gestured wildly at the room around them. "Have you seen my facilities? I'm not exactly fully equipped here. The operation required sending the patient to a hospital - that's how every other Carrier has been dealt with at this Sanctuary. The patient was sent back to her lodgings, and told to wait until a transfer was arranged. Her escape was not my fault."

"You shouldn't have told her what was happening. You should have just arranged the transfer and kept her confined to your clinic until it arrived."

The doctor stared at her, eyes widening with bewilderment. "Are you seriously that stupid? The test she had to do - it doesn't take a genius to work out what that's for. And where am I supposed to keep her when I have other patients to deal with? I've only got the one bed."

"Standard procedure is that a Carrier should be confined until the situation is dealt with," Hawthorne said, maintaining her firm and commanding tone. Unlike this doctor, she wasn't going to let emotion affect her decorum. "If you were unable to hold her here, you should have informed security and they would have placed her under guard."

"I did," the doctor said. "But I was told your troops were too busy with a training exercise, and they would check on the Wandless at intervals throughout the night. So I sent her home. Is it my fault they let her slip out of a window or something?"

Hawthorne grimaced, fighting back her frustration. "Did you tell her she would be placed under guard? It wouldn't surprise me."

"Of course not. This isn't the first time I've handled this."

The woman retrieved her chair and sat behind her desk, rearranging some papers. "Is there anything I can actually help you with, Captain? Or did you simply come here to shift the blame?"

Hawthorne took a step towards her. "Don't take that tone with me. I'm merely trying to ascertain the facts needed to track this witch down."

"Well, you have them," the doctor said. "She came here of her own will, complaining of pains and nausea. Having established she was a Carrier, I contacted the hospital to arrange the operation and security to arrange a guard. As I said, I've done my part."

With that, she picked up a pen and busied herself with her paperwork. Hawthorne glared at her silently for a moment, but was ignored. She turned on the spot and marched smartly towards the door. Just as she grabbed the handle, she looked back at the doctor over her shoulder.

"If that Wandless uses her powers to harm anyone, and I find out you or anyone else in this Sanctuary helped her escape, there will be consequences."

The doctor looked up at her. "Don't try and sugarcoat it, Captain. She's a Carrier - her power has nothing to do with it."

Hawthorne sneered. "You're not one of those witch-lovers, are you?"

The doctor's face remained neutral and focused on her forms. "Would I be working here if I was?"

"I doubt you'll be working here much longer either way."

And before the doctor could respond, Hawthorne yanked the door open and stepped out into the corridor. With a few purposeful strides, she reached the exit and left the building.

The cool air stung her cheek, but she endured it, her

mind whirring, deciding how best to proceed. As satisfying as arguing with the doctor had been, it hadn't brought her any closer to discovering where the Carrier had fled to. Soldiers were scouring the local countryside and towns, but the Wandless had escaped almost twelve hours ago - there was little to no chance she would be within a hundred miles of the Sanctuary.

That cast an impossibly wide net for her troops to search, but they had additional units to call upon in other Sanctuaries and AMSF barracks across the country. The witch would never be far from armed resistance - the captain just needed to know where to send it.

She wandered along the pavement down the winding streets of the Sanctuary, past cottages in which other Wandless inmates had been temporarily locked. She could hear whimpering through some windows as her men interrogated those that knew the Carrier, but the pathetic protestations of innocence drifting through the air sounded maddeningly genuine.

Another sound joined this miserable symphony; hasty but focused footsteps, as if someone was trying to run while still marching. The captain turned to see the lieutenant the Sanctuary had assigned her, a young man whose name she had yet to memorise, striding towards her.

"Captain," he called. "She's been spotted."

6

The rugged terrain slowed the compact car's progress, but there was still progress. The constrained morning sun, shielded by a sheet of cloud, hung to Emilia's right, assuring her that she was travelling north. North-ish. The wheels groaned as they contended with uneven ground, occasionally accompanied by a worrying clatter: cold, hard earth striking the undercarriage. Emilia's already exhausted muscles ached as she tensed against the turbulent rocking of the car, eyes desperately darting back and forth to find flatter routes forward. There were none.

Suddenly, the car lurched down and to the right. With a terrifying crunch, it came to a halt, the engine still growling in defiance. The forceful stop threw her forward, her head bashing against the steering wheel. She raised a hand to her forehead as she sat back in her chair and pulled it away after a moment. No sign of blood, but she could feel bruising beginning at the point of impact. Yet again, Emilia wished she was one of the witchkind blessed with healing magic. There wasn't much left of her that didn't hurt or yearn to rest. How long had it been since she last slept? Almost certainly more than twenty-four hours, and there would be little chance of respite before sundown.

The car had fallen into a pothole - or at least the driver-side front wheel had - that she hadn't seen coming. She put the car into reverse, but the tyres just slipped in the mud and her position remained unchanged. She was alone, without the support or strength to push the car back out. She wanted to stop, to rest, to break down and cry in frustration, but there was no time. She opened the door, swivelled to place her feet out into the field and willed herself to stand.

The cold grasped at her, a gentle but constant breeze chilling her skin. The hidden sun offered little warmth. The drop in temperature woke her up and the solution to her problem became obvious. Denied her powers for so long, it was easy to forget they had returned.

Without even turning to face the car, Emila closed her eyes and connected to it with her mind. One car would be far simpler to move than four quad bikes. She would be on her way in no time. She could feel the vehicle at the edge of her mystical perception but raising an arm to lift it, to coax it into the air, the full weight of what she was trying to do pressed down on her brain. Grunting and roaring in frustration, she raised a second arm, ignoring the splitting pain behind her forehead. The car rattled but still did not move. Emilia braced herself for a third try, but a part of her surrendered - then the rest of her followed. She sank to her knees, no longer able to fight the tears.

Exhaustion, she knew. Nothing more, nothing less. Exhaustion from the night's escape, the emotional day before leaving the Sanctuary, and the never-ending tension of this crisp and cold morning. But exhaustion is simple to identify, and significantly harder to contend with. Magic drew on inner strength, just as much as - if not more than - any physical ability, and required a lot more mental effort. Strength she no longer possessed, effort she just could not manage.

Emilia considered crawling into the back seat of the car and sleeping, just for a few hours, to get her strength back. No, too risky. There was no civilisation for miles around but there were still farms, still the chance that someone would spot a bright blue car sitting in the middle of the field. Still the danger of being discovered while asleep and helpless. Keep running. Or, at the very least, walking.

Turning determinedly north, Emilia pulled the battered coat around her and marched on. Aches and pains rippled across her feet with every step, yet at least it was smoother than the drive. Her eyes locked onto the horizon, and her mind probed as much of the surrounding area as she could with her power. It was a mercy she still had the strength for that.

No one was within range of her power, save for some rather bemused cows who watched her with vague interest as they chewed on grass. She ignored them and pressed on. Briefly she envied them - what would she give to trade places, to have nothing to fear or worry about other than which tuft to next yank out of the ground? The cows eventually grew bored and continued their rhythmic mastication, just as Emilia maintained the steady pace of her feet. Gaps in hedges and open gates allowed her passage from one field to another, and before long the marooned car was a distant blur in the back of her mind as she probed the landscape around her.

Through her power, she became aware of the change in terrain before she saw it. The fields came to an abrupt end just a few minutes walk ahead of her, and relief surged through her as she realised why. The River Tweed, the geographical border between this part of England and Scotland. She had no idea how to cross it, but having the chance to try drove her forward.

Soon she could see where the grass dipped away, black

water flowing past. It swept gently from left to right, but people had tried to swim across this river before and been swept away by a deceptive current. Emilia looked up and down the bank, debating whether to find a narrower or shallower place to cross but the river maintained its width as far as she could see. If she ventured east, she ran the risk of drawing near to Tweedmouth again. West, and she might waste precious hours searching for a safer crossing that didn't exist.

She approached the water. The grass on this side petered out and was replaced by damp and stony earth that squelched beneath her timid footsteps. She stopped at the very edge, the water lapping against her flat and tattered Sanctuary-issued shoes. Once again, she found herself wishing for a different power; there was talk of some witchkind who could will themselves into the air, repel the ground or something that basically enabled them to float.

The desire for other powers had once confused her. For the past few years, Emilia had wished she had no magic at all, that she was - for want of a better term - normal. Back at the Sanctuary, no-one discussed their abilities. At first, it had attracted trouble from the guards, some of whom misconstrued moments of reflection as ambitions for rebellion. Eventually, both the guards and the Wandless mellowed on the matter, but talking about their powers still seemed taboo - perhaps because it was a sharp reminder of why they were there in the first place.

She was procrastinating. The river before her was not becoming any tamer. Time to cross. Emilia put everything to the back of her mind, even the nagging sensory updates from her rekindled power, and focused on the short but dangerous crossing ahead. Stepping into the water sent cold chills racing up her leg and then spine. As her feet submerged beneath the freezing water, it was almost painful, but also revitalising, centring her attention on the task at hand. The sensation increased as she took another step forward, and another, and another. Before long, Emilia was waist deep in the water.

The bed of the river was soft and her feet sank a little with every step, making it harder to prise them out as she pulled forward. The pull of the current increased, desperate to drag her away to the east. She glanced back at the bank; it was only a short distance away but the water level was already rising to her chest. Cold gripped her as tightly as her sodden clothes. Each step took more effort. By the time she was a third of the way across, only her shoulders and head broke the surface.

Emilia stopped only for a second but the pain stretched the moment. If she trudged on, the water would rise above her mouth, possibly her nose, and she would have to swim - but risk getting swept away by the current. Or she could swim now, and risk getting swept away by the current. The water was too cold for her to spend long pondering. Emilia launched herself forward.

The bank before her slid away to the left as the river drove her on towards Tweedmouth. Panic and splashing around made little difference. Stronger, more determined strokes made minimal progress - but there was definitely progress. Emilia channelled all strength into her extremities, ignoring the cold and the pain throughout the rest of her body. Kicking and splashing at the water, the bank slowly drew closer. It rushed past and she had already travelled several metres away from where she first entered the water but it was definitely getting closer.

The weight of her clothes pressed upon her, almost as oppressive as the current. She tentatively lowered her foot to the river bed but it was still slightly out of reach and she dipped under the water. Spluttering as the icy liquid burned her mouth and throat, she took a few more strokes and the bank drew even nearer.

Emilia reached down with her leg again, this time connecting to soft but gloriously sturdy mud. She lowered the other to meet it and stood. The water slapped at her chin, the current still pushing against her, but she had regained control. Her steps became easier and more confident as she left the strongest part of the current behind. The air chilled any skin that rose above the water and the cruel wind passed straight through her soaked clothing.

Soon her waist, then her knees burst free from the river and she found herself striding with joy and relief onto the opposite side. Cold, wet, exhausted but back on dry land. Welcome to Scotland.

7

The captain had spent the entire journey to Tweedmouth in silence, as had her lieutenant. As the train neared the station - it had worked out faster than driving, given the distance they needed to travel - Hawthorne stood and marched towards the sliding doors, the younger officer behind her. The very moment the gap was wide enough, she stepped onto the platform.

The air this close to the Scottish border was colder, teasing goosebumps from the skin of her arms, but she ignored them, just as she ignored the civilians crowding on the platform ready to board the train. Recognising the black uniform, the people parted like a biblical sea for the two officers and within moments, she was through the barrier and onto the concourse.

Outside the station, they were greeted by a line of six soldiers, three cars forming a row behind them.

"Welcome to Tweedmouth, Captain," the man on the far left said, saluting. "I'm Sergeant..."

"Who authorised this?" Hawthorne snapped.

The sergeant blinked, his words catching in his throat. "I... er... it was..."

"Doesn't matter. This is a waste of precious time and resources. It does not require six soldiers to greet two officers. Not when there's a rogue Wandless on the loose. Which one is the car I ordered?"

The sergeant turned to look, grimaced at this unnecessary gesture, and nodded. "The first one, Captain," he said, and sheepishly handed over the keys.

"Good," she said, snatching them out of his hand and marching towards the car. "Resume the search. Concentrate on the surrounding areas, but particularly on any potential border crossing. The Carrier is likely to have made a break for the North."

"Yes, Captain. Right away, Captain."

The sergeant fumbled a salute and climbed clumsily into his car. The others followed suit. The lieutenant made for the driver's door, but Hawthorne overtook him and climbed in, huffing as she watched him scurry round the bonnet and climb into the passenger seat. The two cars behind them rumbled into life and drove away.

"Do you have the address, Lieutenant?" she asked, driving off before he had even fastened his seat belt.

"Yes, Captain," the lieutenant replied, leaning forward to enter it into the vehicle's satnav system. There was a musical chime, and a recorded female voice provided the first instructions.

"Captain, may I ask..." the lieutenant began, but faltered.

"What?" Hawthorne barked. "If you're going to ask a question, commit. You've already seen how I feel about time wasters."

The lieutenant straightened, his voice taking on a much more efficient tone. "Captain, are you sure it was necessary to come all the way here yourself? This is just one sighting, and it's a long way from the Sanctuary. Could we not have sent..."

"It's not just one sighting, Lieutenant," Hawthorne said, never taking her eyes off the road. "It's the only sighting.

We had no leads back at the Sanctuary, so if there's even a chance of catching up to her and cutting her off, I'm going to take it."

"But how would she have got this far north?"

"Plenty of ways. She might have stolen a vehicle, she might have had transport arranged by friends or those blind morons at Free The Wandless..."

"Actually," the lieutenant interrupted, but in such an authoritative tone Hawthorne found herself less irritated than she normally would, "the organisation issued a statement this morning claiming they had nothing to do with the escape, and even offered to assist in the search."

Hawthorne snorted. "Course they did. Puts them in a position to hinder our efforts."

"I think they're more keen to ensure we take the Wandless in alive, Captain," the lieutenant replied, "after that Carrier was shot by Captain Wilkington six years back."

"I don't care if this one ends up dead or alive - just that she's stopped. You saw what she did to the troops who first chased her - and that was within minutes of leaving the suppression field. Who knows how powerful she'll be at full strength - let alone her powers amplified as a Carrier."

"I thought studies had failed to definitively prove that has any effect." Hawthorne shot him a look.

"Do you really want to take that chance? We let this Carrier escape, or even an ordinary Wandless, and who knows what havoc they could wreak? They could gather enough support to take down a suppression field, liberate a Sanctuary, start an uprising. They could use their increased power to assault AMSF facilities, assassinate members of the government, commit mass slaughter. They could unravel the very fabric of society."

"You really think one witch could do all that?"

"It won't be just one. We let one Carrier escape and others will follow. Any witchkind might attempt their own breaks for freedom. And then what happens? Everything we've worked to build in the last nine years is undone. This is not about one witch. This is about protecting England from another Harwich."

"That was one incident, Captain," the lieutenant said. "A long time ago. The Sanctuary system, the new laws - they've all prevented that from happening. Even if this one Wandless were to get away, I doubt it would be that serious."

"That's because you weren't there," Hawthorne said, glancing over at him through narrowed eyes. "You didn't see what they can do."

8

Sergeant Hawthorne had to admit she was surprised at how many Wandless turned up. Word had spread of this protest over the past few weeks, but it was the easiest thing in the world to share the news on LifeStream or stick a flyer to your car window. Actually attending, physically expressing your defiance against the law, took a lot more courage. And stupidity.

The crowd's chants seemed passionate enough, the slogans on their placards were catchy, but this protest was foolhardy. For a start, there was no media here to televise it - largely because Hawthorne had ordered her men to physically remove those who had been here when they arrived, and any that had appeared since were held back by the widest perimeter she had been able to set up.

Also, as with so many demonstrations throughout the nation's history, the protesters seemed to massively overestimate their influence on the law. The proposed Sanctuary system was a dead cert to get through Parliament, particularly after that Wandless had murdered his local MP. It would just need one more death at the hands of witchkind to tip the government over the edge. Hawthorne felt - no, knew - that was inevitable.

Perhaps the one thing the protesters did get right was

their choice of location. Shutting down the Harwich International Port would certainly get the government's attention; flooding the streets of the capital outside Parliament was frustrating for the law-makers inside, but disrupting trade and travel had far more impact. The other protests around the country - Hull, Liverpool, Dover, Portsmouth, and even one of the major London airports - would amplify their message. The economical impact of a single day's blocked trade would be felt for weeks or longer if these activists dug in and stayed put.

Hawthorne made a mental note to investigate which port employee had allowed this rabble to take over Harwich, and suggest her colleagues in the other regions did the same. That was the danger that witchkind posed: they could be anywhere. They were embedded in society, and no one knew just what they were capable of. Sanctuaries would solve that.

The leader of the protest was rambling on about their cause, warning the police to keep their distance, but there was no real threat in his words. When Hawthorne and her men had first arrived, he had asked them to show support, show compassion and even join in with their demonstration but had quickly realised from the intimidating formation the sergeant had arranged that this plea was in vain.

As the leader continued his rallying cry, occasionally interrupted by a cheer or roar of agreement from his flock, Hawthorne realised how his words carried so easily across the port towards her. The man held a hand to his own neck, as if preparing to strangle himself, and his voice echoed between the cargo containers as if projected by a megaphone. Magic. It just wasn't needed, wasn't natural. And while that particular power didn't seem too dangerous, there was no telling what else the man could do. Perhaps he could make his voice so loud it would deafen her men, shatter glass, or even topple the containers around them. The very thought made Hawthorne tighten her grip on the pistol at her hip.

Movement drew her attention away from the orator. A cluster of four Wandless were cutting through the crowd, starting somewhere in the middle and moving to the very edge. Even from this distance, Hawthorne could see a different determination on their faces. With the rest of the protestors, it was almost passive, as if yelling slogans and waving signs was enough to change the world. But these four clearly had something more active in mind.

The similarities in facial structure and hairline suggested they might be related, and they moved almost in perfect sync, as if this were rehearsed. The man leading them broke away, heading for the front of the crowd where the amplified leader stood, while the woman and two girls - his wife and daughters? - strode purposefully towards the police. Hawthorne kept them in her peripheral vision, but watched as the man grasped the protest leader's wrist and held it to his own neck, as if asking to be strangled.

"Brothers and sisters," he called, his voice now echoing across the port. "The time for talking is over. They won't listen. They won't even allow the people to listen - look how they sent away the news crews so no one would hear our protests."

The hairs on Hawthorne's back rose. Without turning, she told the men either side of her to ready their weapons but to hold fire until her command.

"We may not outnumber them," the man continued, holding the other's hand firm despite his struggles. "But we are more powerful than they could possibly imagine, and that terrifies them. We are the superior species, so why should we let them decide our future? Drop those signs, and use your God-given magic instead. Don't ask for your freedom, take it. Fight back."

At this, he wrenched the man's hand away from his throat and turned to follow his family, already halfway between the protestors and the police. The leader fell to the ground. As he tried to stand, he clasped his hand to his neck and bellowed desperately in the direction of the police.

"Please," he cried. "This man doesn't speak for us. We don't want any violence. We don't want - "

But violence had already been unleashed.

The two girls, unquestionably sisters from this distance, raised their hands, each crackling with power. The girl on the left glowed orange as fire engulfed her fists, and before Hawthorne knew was was happening, flames danced wildly towards her front line. Simultaneously, the girl on the right thrust her hands forward, fingers splayed like claws, glowing electric blue. Lighting lashed out towards them, striking faster than she could blink. Without wands, neither sister seemed to have control of the power they unleashed. Neither seemed to care.

To Hawthorne's right, men fell to the ground. To her left, they screamed in pain as the flames licked their flesh, uniforms catching alight. Instinctively, the sergeant dropped to the ground, drawing her pistol in one smooth movement as she did so. She landed prone, the pistol held out before her. She yelled as she pulled the trigger.

"Fire!"

Gunshots cut through the roar of the flames and the crackle of lightning. In the distance, Hawthorne could hear screams of confusion from the protestors. Both the panicked voices and chattering weaponry suddenly grew louder as the magical assault ceased. The smoke cleared and Hawthorne saw the three women standing there, now joined by the man. The mother held her arms out either side, palms upward, her face a picture of strained effort despite the seemingly relaxed pose.

Hawthorne's men had stopped firing in the confusion, guns still trained on the family of four. The sergeant stood, aimed for the mother and fired. Her single shot echoed between the cargo containers, but the mother did not flinch. The bullet ricocheted off thin air and slammed into the ground. Hawthorne snarled and unleashed the rest of the clip at the family, but every shot suddenly diverted. The rest of the policemen took her cue and began firing rapidly, but their bullets were blocked by the same unseen barrier.

Most battered the ground in front of the Wandless. Some whizzed up into the air. One bounced off the right side of the shield and caught the leader of the protest in the chest. The police stopped firing as they watched the man slump to the ground, his already lifeless eyes frozen in a look of pain and confusion.

The father of the family spoke, his voice muffled slightly by the invisible field but loud enough to be heard.

"You see? Our lives mean nothing to them. What do they mean to you?"

It didn't take long. Some of the protestors - mostly men, the sergeant noticed - raised their hands, fingers in claw-like formations, shoulders set into a more aggressive pose. One man to the left of the crowd began running towards the police, making a show of how deeply he was inhaling. A few of the officers he faced panicked and began firing again, but the Wandless man stopped and opened his mouth, breathing out dramatically. Hawthorne felt a sudden and strong gust of wind, but it was nothing compared to what her men were subjected to. The man's powerful exhalation toppled several of her officers, their streams of gunfire ceasing or diverting up into the air.

The sergeant turned her weapon towards him but a rush of movement distracted her. The family of four had resumed their attack, more Wandless protestors had joined them, and those who hadn't were scurrying about in distress, hoping to find a way around the police line and back to safety.

Sergeant Hawthorne fired wherever she had a clean shot. Wandless and police officers alike were dropping around her. She risked glances at the family as she tried to target the mother and father but the sisters and other witchkind rebels got in her way. The sound of magic, gunfire and screams faded into white noise until Hawthorne was convinced she could hear the determined throbbing of her own heart. She used it as a rhythm to which she ducked, wove and punched her way through the mob that had formed around her, shoving back any Wandless that weren't already wrestling with her men.

Scuffling combatants bumped her back and forth, the heat of spells blasted at her skin, but she maintained her course towards the four wretches who had started this. One of the sisters saw her coming and fired lightning in her direction, but Hawthorne recognised the flamboyant arm movement of an imminent yet arrogant attack and ducked just in time. As she dove to the ground, she raised an arm and fired. Her bullet tore through the sister's leg, unleashing a yowl of pain and the girl fell.

As she did, the mother appeared, her back to the sergeant. Reflexes kicked in, Hawthorne swung her arm towards her target, squeezing the trigger as soon as she was in line. The woman's head jerked to the side as the shot buried into her skull.

The sisters screamed in unison, alerting the father. Even from this distance, Hawthorne could see his body shaking with rage, nostrils flaring, eyes glaring. Glaring at her. She swung her gun towards him as she tried to stand, but he was already running towards her, one hand outstretched. The pistol shifted in Hawthorne's hand, almost slipping from her grasp. She tightened her grip, but the weapon fought back, pulling itself towards the Wandless father. She squeezed the trigger, but he somehow sensed the path of the bullets and ducked to the side. Then the trigger jammed, held in place by some unknown force.

Hawthorne brought her other hand up to the gun, but it wrestled free of her grip and flew towards the father. He caught it effortlessly and casually tossed it aside, never losing momentum as he advanced on her. She could see his calculating eyes planning a myriad of deaths for her, and clenched her fists ready to meet him, matching his determined stance.

The man slowed and stopped, realisation dawning on his face along with a chilling smile. He stood just a few feet away from her and raised his arms grandly either side of him. There was a spine-curling creak of metal. Most of the combatants - Wandless and police alike - ceased their struggles, heads turning wildly to identify where the noise came from. The unholy sound screamed through the air again, and Hawthorne caught movement in the corner of her eye. Dozens of people turned towards the colossal cargo containers that towered over them. There was a sharp grind of metal on metal, then screams.

Two containers, one either side of the protest, shifted. They shuffled forwards, and rose into the air. Hawthorne looked back at the father, who grinned wickedly at her. As he raised his hands further over his head and brought them together, the containers matched his movements, casting a shadow over the crowd. Hawthorne felt cold as the sun's light left her. Cold and afraid.

She was vaguely aware of another voice, a man to her left, shouting a command. Then gunfire sounded from all directions and the father jerked and spasmed as each shot penetrated. He fell to the ground, and the containers came with him. The ground shook as they landed, knocking Hawthorne and others back to the floor. The terrified screams of those beneath the containers were suddenly silenced, replaced by a wet crunch the sergeant would never forget.

The gunfire continued.

For all their magic, the Wandless were powerless against bullets. With their shield and their leader gone, the family fell, although not before burning, electrifying and murdering many of the good men and women around Hawthorne. It took five men each to gun down the sisters.

Some of the witchkind had fought on regardless. They, too, now lay lifeless on the ground. Others stood down, hands raised in fear and surrender. Those who had not fought back cowered in a circle, at least seven guns trained on them. Hawthorne idly wondered where her superiors would find enough cells to contain them all.

9

The sun had slid into its mid-afternoon position before Emilia saw any form of civilisation. While the road that ran parallel with the Tweed on England's side had only been a short distance from the river, the nearest Scottish lane was easily several miles north of the water. Even when she reached it, there were no signs of vehicles, no passing hikers, no indication that any human beings - or witchkind - had passed that way in a long time.

The wind had dried most of her clothes but they no longer offered the warmth and comfort they once had. She could already feel the cold creeping into her bones, the onset of nausea and she wondered if her magic - or her other concern - would be affected.

From what little she could remember of the map she studied back at the Sanctuary, the nearest main road to where she thought she was lay to the West, so Emilia headed east. She was in no state to tackle the AMSF or whatever Scottish authorities they might be working with. Both her muscles and mind ached, dizzy spells disoriented her as she walked, and she began to feel disconnected from her regained magic, as if the exhaustion powered an internal suppression field.

After almost an hour of walking along the lane, she saw

it: a thin pillar of smoke twirling into the air above the hedge to the left. It could only be a chimney, which meant shelter, warmth, perhaps even food. Just the very thought triggered a pang of hunger and she pressed on. Sure enough, a gap in the hedge appeared near the smoke's origin and as she limped closer, she saw it housed a short wooden gate. The latch lifted easily, more to prevent the gate from blowing around in the wind than actually provide security, and she stepped onto the narrow gravel path beyond.

The cottage was compact but welcoming, its whitewashed walls hinting at a neutrality she prayed its owners shared. Either side of the path were lovingly tended rose bushes, complimented by the occasional stone pot bearing more vibrant plants. The gravel diverged into three pathways, two leading either side of the building and the third directly to the yellow wooden door. Emilia's survival instinct overrode the urge to knock and she snuck down the left path. The gravel betrayed her presence. She tried to step more carefully and slowly, but the crunch was inescapable. Her eyes flicked to the windows searching for any sign of movement, but so far she remain unnoticed. The relief spurred her on, and she was just rounding the corner of the cottage when she heard the voice.

"Who the hell are you?" he said, his accent heavy and aggressive. "What're you doing in our garden?"

Emilia turned to face the owner of the cottage. The man was tall, and much older than her, but sturdily built. A brown cardigan, thick woollen shirt and jeans protected him from the cold. The rolling pin, presumably the only weapon he could find, was held aloft to protect his home.

"P-please sir," she stammered. "I'm lost. I was just looking for shelter and somewhere to rest."

"You're English?" he said, eyebrow raising, rolling pin

still held firm.

"Yes. I'm trying to get to Edinburgh. Thought I'd take the scenic route after crossing the border but my car slipped into a ditch. I couldn't get it out, and I've been walking for hours." The weight of the true ordeal threatened to overwhelm her as she spoke. "Please, I'm so tired and I just need... I need..."

"Hmm."

He lowered the rolling pin, resting the other end in his free hand, keeping it accessible. Brow furrowing, he looked her up and down. She could feel his eyes scrutinising her body - not in the lewd way some men were known to do but it still sent a chill through her skin.

"You look like you fell in a river."

"Yes, sir. I... it was a pond back down the road," she said, suddenly remembering the one she had passed and pointing that way. "I was kneeling to scoop up some water. I needed a drink, but I leaned too far and..."

Emilia tailed off as she lost confidence in the lie. His reaction was instant, but not the one she expected.

He burst out laughing.

"You tried drinking out of that?" he snorted. "Are you mad, girl? You any idea how many cows piss and shite in that?"

"Well, I..." A smile began to form on her face. The first laugh she had heard in days, perhaps weeks. There wasn't much to laugh about at the Sanctuary.

"Oh, and you must've looked a right sight as you went in," he said, triggering another bout of laughter. He wiped the beginning of a tear from his eye. "I wish I'd seen it."

The arm with the rolling pin dropped to his side and he extended a hand. Emilia's heart burst at the invitation and without thinking, she took it.

"Come on," he said. "Let's get you all warmed up. We'll

get you fed, too – try to put some fat on that bony little frame of yours."

He led the fugitive back around the front of the cottage and through the open door. A world of warmth enveloped her, and tears began to form. The heat of the roaring log fire across the room embraced her, reaching every inch of her skin, triggering an involuntary sigh of relief.

Her host closed the door, shutting out the last hints of the cold world beyond and Emilia felt safer than she had in years. A small voice at the back of her mind urged her to remain attentive, to remember she didn't know this man or his stance on witchkind, but the rest of her was so grateful for warmth, mirth and kindness that good sense was easily silenced.

"Take a seat," the man said, gesturing towards an armchair disguised by a hand-knitted throw. Emilia did not hesitate. She marched over to the chair with newfound strength and collapsed into it. The cushions sank farther than she expected, the throw hugging her arms and legs, and the tension in her muscles disappeared in an instant.

"Thank you," she said, fighting the tears.

"No problem. I'm Rory, by the by. Welcome to Highland Cottage."

"Eve," she replied, a smile disguising her most comfortable lie. "Pleased to meet you."

"I'll go stick the kettle on. You just sit there and relax."

Even if she wanted to, Emilia didn't have the strength to argue. She rested her head against the back of the armchair, and watched the hypnotic flames beneath the thick oak mantelpiece. They danced invitingly, as if putting on a show to distract from her worries, and the constant barrage of heat soothed her once stinging cheeks. Emilia's eyelids tripled in weight, and she struggled to keep them open. Occasionally, she became aware of darkness all around her and jerked awake. Eventually, she lost the struggle.

10

"She's heading for Scotland," Hawthorne said as she marched into the musty warmth of the computer lab. "I need to know why."

"Yes, Captain," the lieutenant said, carefully edging past her and taking a seat at one of the two unmanned computers. "I'll start with her government profile, see if there's a detail we missed."

"Good," said Hawthorne, turning to the rest of the room. There were long benches of desks with computers, sixteen in all, each with an analyst already clattering away on the keyboard. The Tweedmouth commander had loaned her this intel force - she just hoped they were more competent than the men she had dealt with so far.

The waitress at the café had confirmed Harris was in the area, but had been unable to offer any more useful information. The Wandless had paid in cash, probably found in the stolen car, and had not interacted with anyone. No meetings at the café, no phone calls, nothing to indicate why she had travelled this far north - other than the assumption she was trying to cross the border.

The sergeant who greeted her unnecessarily at the station had then called to report his team had found the car. Abandoned in a field, it had indeed borne traces of the

Carrier - fingerprints, strands of hair, and so on - and had quite clearly been driving towards the river that marked the English-Scottish border. But the fact that it had taken the local troops so long to find it, given how close to the town it was, or that the commander hadn't thought to implement more thorough border defences in light of the crisis beggared belief.

She cleared her throat and every head - aside from the lieutenant's - snapped towards her, awaiting instruction.

"The Carrier has escaped across the border into Scotland," she said. "Central command is already negotiating with Scottish forces to share resources in our search and allow an acceptable number of our own troops across the border to assist in her arrest. Or elimination. These negotiations are expected to be complete within the next two hours - I want a destination by then. I want to know where she's heading and why. Look for past connections, known contacts, local Wandless sympathisers, absolutely anything. I don't want guesses, I want probable explanations. Working theories based on evidence. Chop chop."

She clapped her hands for emphasis and the air filled with frenzied typing. Hawthorne walked over to the empty desk by the lieutenant.

"Anything so far?" she asked as she opened a browser on her own machine.

"Nothing obvious. Harris, Emilia. Born in Suffolk. All previous known addresses were in Suffolk or Essex."

"Parents?"

The lieutenant clicked a few links. "Same. Well, mother was from Norfolk, but still East Anglian. They're both still living in Suffolk, although they appear to have separated. Not sure when."

"Any siblings?"

More clicks. "An older brother, but he died at Harwich."

Hawthorne turned. "Was he witchkind too?"

"No," the lieutenant replied. "She's the only one in the family. He seems to have just been supporting his sister and her cause."

"Then good riddance," the captain sneered, turning back to her own search. She paused for a moment and looked at the officer. "Lieutenant, carry on with the Carrier's previous movements. Find out if she's ever been north of the border."

The search continued, but few connections to Scotland emerged. Emilia Harris had never lived there, spent a significant amount of time there, checked in there via social media, applied for a Scottish visa, worked for a company with Scottish owners or interests, or seemingly interacted with many people from the nation in any meaningful way. It was maddening.

Delving into Harris' internet history, one analyst had found several conversations between her and forum members or social media users who turned out to be based in and around Scotland, but none of these gleaned any sort of personal connection. Harris had never exchanged addresses or contact information with these users, and there seemed to be no indication she even knew some of them were based in Scotland.

Someone contacted the Sanctuary where she had been held and arranged remote access to her private communications - email, archive of scanned physical mail, and so on - but nothing there had any link to the DRS. Most of it was everyday messages between Harris and her parents, spaced out every few months. This was unsurprising - the Wandless had soon become aware their messages were all being closely monitored, so few truly opened up in them or disclosed anything personal.

Communication beyond their Sanctuaries was essentially checking in, an emotionless affair.

There were rumours some witchkind had found ways to communicate by magical means with people outside the Sanctuaries, but Hawthorne refused to believe them. She had thoroughly investigated each one, of course - if there was even the slightest chance Wandless could be coordinating with the outside world, it needed to be stopped. The fact that breakouts were few and far between, and that no mass riot or escape had been orchestrated, assured her that the rumours were just that. No, less than that. Naive hope.

"Aha!" cried one analyst at the far side of the room. There was a violent scrape as Hawthorne shoved her chair back and marched smartly over to where the woman was sitting.

"What have you got?" she said, but looking at the screen gave her that answer.

Emilia Harris - a much younger Emilia Harris - could be seen standing in the stone courtyard in front of Edinburgh Castle. The animated photo was on a three-second loop, with Harris and another woman, one even younger, cracking into cheesy smiles before laughing together. The crisp blue sky, dazzling sun and puffy coats the two women wore suggested this was taken in winter but there was no other indication as to when this had occurred.

"Where did you find this?" Hawthorne asked, leaning in to scrutinise the image for further clues.

"One of her earliest photos on LifeStream," the analyst replied. "Judging by other photos posted the same day, I'd say she was only in Edinburgh for about 24 hours. Maybe 48. Probably flew up one day and back the next."

"Why didn't it show up that she had applied for a visa, even a visiting one?"

"The photos are dated fifteen years ago, just before the visa requirement was put in place."

Hawthorne stood and frowned. "Who's the woman?"

"Not sure. She hasn't been tagged on LifeStream."

"Facial recognition search?"

The analyst shook her head. "Nothing came up. She doesn't appear to be on the English database. She might be a Scot, but we won't be able to access their database without permission. I imagine we'll get that if they join us in the search."

"Are there more photos of the two of them together?"

The woman nodded and clicked to minimise the photo, scrolling further up the feed. As she came across more relevant pictures, she would briefly maximise them to full screen, then minimise and move on to the next. In each photo, Harris and the woman appeared to be close, meeting every six to nine months. In fact, the visits only seem to have stopped when Harris was arrested.

"If the visas came in after that Edinburgh visit, and that woman's a Scot, how can they have met so frequently?"

"Could be the Scot came down here. Could be that it was easier to arrange an English visa for one person rather than Scottish for two."

The captain frowned again. "Two people?"

The analyst tapped the screen. "Whoever's taking this picture - or more importantly the one in Edinburgh. All photos of these two are taken from a distance, so there's a third party involved."

Hawthorne's skin tingled. Finally, they were onto something. She could feel it.

"Find this woman. Find out who took these photos. Find out everything you can."

"Yes, Captain," the analyst replied, and began frantically typing and clicking to continue her search.

Hawthorne marched back to her own desk and tried to pick up the thread she had been working on, but in her heart she already knew it was a dead end. This mystery woman seemed to be the best lead.

"Any luck back there?" the lieutenant asked, not looking away from his screen.

"Could be," the captain said. "We've found a woman, probably Scottish, who was meeting with the Carrier regularly before she was arrested. No idea who she is yet, but we'll find her."

"Uh-huh," the lieutenant replied, distracted by his own monitor. They worked in silence for a moment before he spoke again.

"Captain," he said, this single word rising in pitch with hopeful confidence. "I think I've found her."

11

"What the hell is she doing here, Rory?" another voice cried, higher in tone but just as aggressive.

Emilia's eyes snapped open, her head jerked upwards, and her neck ached from the awkward chin-to-chest angle it had been in. She had no idea how long she had been asleep, but the dimming light passing through the window meant it had been well over an hour.

The man standing at the front door glared at her with dark eyes and even darker eyebrows. His three-piece suit gave him an air of authority that quickly rendered her speechless, gripped by an instinctive fear, and she felt powerless as he marched over. He towered above her, nostrils flaring, and inhaled as he prepared to bellow.

"Wait, Callum" Rory called, scurrying in from another room. "I invited her."

"I would hope so if she's in our living room," the other man scoffed, "but it doesn't answer my question. What the hell is she doing here?"

"Her name's Eve," Rory said, stepping up and gently pushing the man back with an open hand. "She got lost after her car got stuck in a ditch, and she just needs shelter and a little food. There's no one around for miles, so I figured we're the only ones who can help her."

"She's not Eve," Callum growled. "I know perfectly well who she is."

A chill ran through the Wandless, far colder and more distressing than the river she had waded through.

"*She,* my dear husband, is why you should watch the news once in a while. *She* is a Wandless. She escaped from her Sanctuary last night, killed four guards and has the entirety of the English's witch-hunting forces after her. She is probably the most wanted person within 100 miles - and definitely the most dangerous. She is Emilia Harris."

"That's ridiculous," Rory said, but Emilia could hear his doubts.

Callum never broke eye contact with her, his brown eyes gleaming with anger. Were her blue irises the shining pools of innocence that she hoped? A cold breeze through the open front door punctuated the moment, prompting the taller man to end the silence.

"She's dangerous," Callum repeated.

Emilia frowned and stood, drawing on her power. Taken aback, Callum retreated a step or two, his arms instinctively raising to block an attack he couldn't possibly defend against.

"You're right," she said, trying to sound as menacing as possible. With a mere flick of her hand, the door slammed shut. "I am dangerous."

"Rory," said Callum, his voice weaker. "Get out, get help."

Even without taking her eyes off Callum, Emilia could see Rory was frozen to the spot. It took him a moment to work up the courage to step towards the kitchen door. The Wandless raised a hand, but more as a gesture of reassurance than a threat.

"Rory, wait," she said. "I mean you no harm. I can be dangerous, but that's not why they're chasing me. Callum,

I really am lost and in need of help. I know what they're saying about me, but the truth is..."

She sat back in the armchair, bracing herself.

"I'm pregnant."

The two lines had glared at her, each one a pillar of judgment. Emilia met their gaze, but it was hard to show strength when the test that carried them quivered in her trembling hands.

She had known it was always possible - expected it, in fact. It was why she had requested to see Dr Collins in the first place. Her complaints of nausea, fatigue and cramps were genuine, but claims that she didn't know the cause? That had all been a lie.

Collins' shrewd but not unkind eyes as she had presented the tray suggested she already knew. Despite the range of needles, swabs, thermometers and other medical implements she had gathered, it was Emilia's reaction to the pregnancy test that the doctor had scrutinised the most. No, Emilia was certain the woman understood the situation more than she had let on. Why wouldn't she? She was a doctor, and a mother herself.

And yet Emilia couldn't bring herself to face her again. Not yet. The bolt locking the toilet door, flimsy as it might be, protected her from the reality of it all. From the consequences.

The temptation to flush the test away, to snap it in two and hide it in the cistern, was intense but it would have told Dr Collins everything the result could. And even if Emilia disposed of it, what then? There was nowhere she could run to elsewhere in the Sanctuary, not without the doctor finding her.

A knock on the door shattered any illusions of escape.

"Emilia? Everything okay in there?"

The doctor did not sound as concerned as she might have thought, but the Wandless were used to her detached manner. Even so, the underlying authority in that voice gripped Emilia's attention, motivating her in a way that, in this moment, she never could.

"Fine," she replied, surprised by the stability of her own voice. Also, the strength of the lie. She was far from fine. "Just took a while for the test to work."

"And?"

As if controlled by another, Emilia rose from where she sat and flicked the bolt across. Before she could even reach for the handle, Dr Collins gently pushed the door open, her eyes already searching for the stick. Emilia lacked the energy to hide it, limply handing it over. The doctor took it and made a good show of looking at it, reading the result thoroughly as if the two lines were some indecipherable symbol from a foreign language.

After a few agonising seconds, she turned and marched back to her office across the corridor, her purposeful stride wordlessly commanding Emilia to follow. For a moment, the Wandless hesitated, as if she were still safe where she stood, protected by the imagined timeless bubble that enveloped the surgery's solitary toilet. She could feel herself leaning to go, her body determined to face the inevitable, but her now pounding head refused, holding her back.

A polite cough from the unseen doctor, whether genuine or forced, snapped her out of it and she walked timidly back to the office. The doctor was already sitting behind her desk, typing determinedly, eyes locked onto the monitor. Emilia sat in the same chair she had occupied just minutes or an eternity ago, and sat in silence.

"So," Collins asked, not looking over, "how did this

happen?"

It wasn't a personal question. The doctor had no interest in the circumstances, just the consequences. Emilia weighed up how much to tell her. She had already debated this for days before booking the appointment but the shock of the result, of having her fears confirmed, left her mind blank.

"Well, I..."

"Did you use protection?" the doctor asked.

"Yes," Emilia replied quickly, then bit her lip.

The Sanctuary shop obviously didn't sell such items - doing so would be seen as encouragement - but the more opportunistic staff members smuggled them in and traded them with the Wandless, often taking what prized possessions they had left. The doctor and guards were well aware that these and other forms of contraband were in circulation, but efforts to cut off this trade had proven to be fruitless.

Emilia braced herself for an interrogation as to where she acquired hers from, but none came. Not the doctor's department, perhaps. Instead, a question she had not even thought to prepare for, despite how obvious it seemed now.

"Who's the father?"

Again there was little to no emotion behind the doctor's words, nor was there any aggression. It was as if the woman was merely reading from a checklist, completely disinterested in the answers. Emilia fought to suppress the image of the man's face from her mind, as if even thinking of him would reveal his identity. A strangely protective mood overcame her, and she clenched her jaw.

"Does it matter?"

The doctor's typing paused, and her eyes flicked up and away from the screen, still not looking at her patient.

"No," she said, "I suppose not."

She finished typing, clicked through a few tasks; no doubt alerting the Sanctuary's governor, or at least someone in his office. Her report completed, Doctor Collins pushed her chair back from the desk a little and swivelled to finally look directly at Emilia.

The weight of the doctor's gaze was too much. Emilia burst into tears. An uncontrollable sobbing took over, and she gasped for breath as she tried to calm herself down. Rational thought still penetrated the emotional rush, but it was not enough to stop the torrent that flowed down her cheeks.

Through blurred vision, Emilia saw concern wash over the doctor's face, a sudden and surreal change from the methodical woman who had directed proceedings so far. She stood and walked round her desk to the shaking witch, grabbing a box of tissues as she did so. She placed the box in Emilia's lap and leant back against her desk.

"You're not in trouble," she said.

Her soft words did more than Emilia's self-control ever could, and the Wandless felt a weight lift from her chest. The torrent slowed, but did not stop. The despair that was gradually dissipating was just as quickly replaced by shame and embarrassment. She had spent days preparing herself for this, the worst outcome. Yet it turned out nothing could prepare her for that moment.

"It's okay," the doctor said. "It happens. You're not the first to come here with the same problem. Despite what you are, you are still human. We can take care of this. It will be as if it never happened."

Something about Collins' choice of words triggered something in Emilia. Strange how a brief moment can instantly alter your perspective, like an anti-climactic first kiss that shatters a long-harboured infatuation. Her once-powerful mind began considering options she had spent many tortured moments dismissing, ambitions she hadn't dared share with anyone.

The image of weakened ground beneath a particular stretch of fence, and the distant treeline she often gazed at from there, fought its way to the forefront of her mind. Somehow, it seemed closer.

She took a tissue and wiped the tears from her eyes.

12

"Why would they be chasing you just because you're pregnant?" Rory asked.

But Callum's mind was two steps ahead, despite its efforts to deny the truth.

"They don't...?" he began.

Emilia opened her mouth to answer but her voice caught in her throat, instead escaping as a quivering squeak and a weak, clipped breath.

"Don't what?" Rory asked, turning to his husband.

Callum never took his eyes off her, but the ferocity of his gaze had diminished. The anger had given way to a reassuring blend of sympathy and pity. "They... terminate Wandless pregnancies, don't they?"

She could only offer a feeble nod in response.

"But I thought not all Wandless children had magic? It's not certain your baby would have any powers."

"They..." Emilia started, but struggled to finish.

Callum did so for her. "They don't want to take the risk. They terminate them anyway."

Rory's dramatic intake of breath would have been comical had it not been laced with horror. He staggered to the side and sat on the arm of a nearby chair. He stared at the floor, eyes glazed over, his thoughts no doubt lost with the many children that would never be born. "That's... barbaric."

The last word sent a spark through Emilia. She herself had never applied that term to the fate of her people, but hearing it from another - and a regular human, especially - somehow validated it. At the Sanctuary, the forced terminations were yet another unspoken truth between the Wandless, much like the nature of their powers before relocation. Their inability to change things effectively negated the need to discuss it. On reflection, perhaps this was why so many imprisoned Wandless only developed friendships with people of the same gender, subconsciously avoiding the opportunity - and danger - of intimacy.

Rory's voice called Emilia back to the scene, his gaze still fixed on the carpet. "But why?"

"They see it as the most humane solution to the problem," she said, disgust increasing with every word. "If they kill all of us, it's genocide. If they let us live out our lives but make sure we don't breed, it's population control. They just want us to die out."

"But this pregnancy was an accident, right?" Callum asked. "If you know that's what they do, why would you try to have a..."

"What the hell has that got to do with anything?" Rory barked, his head snapping towards his husband. "Are you saying Wandless don't have a right to children?"

Callum held up his hands. "That's not what I'm saying at all. Look, I... this is complicated... I'm trying to say this without sounding too offensive, but..."

"But what? What are you trying to say, dear?"

The man's shoulders dropped. "This is going to sound callous, and I honestly don't mean it to, but... The operation is quite simple, it causes no lasting damage to you, so why not go through with it? Surely, it's far more dangerous to escape, go on the run, than it would be for them to just... you know... and then you carry on with your life. As awful as that sounds."

Emilia glanced at Rory, who stared incredulously at his other half. Her host's continued outrage gave her the strength to respond. Incredible how many hard truths you could utter when you know you're not alone.

"Because they would also have terminated... me."

Her words prompted a short and sullen silence as the reality of her situation was thrown into sharp relief. Now it was Callum's turn to gasp, to lose all composure or hint of understanding.

"Why? Why would they kill you?" he asked, voice trembling. "I know you said they would abort the bairn because of the limit England is trying to put on witchkind, population control and all that. But why would they need to kill you?"

Emilia grimaced. The conversation was bringing up topics that she and her fellow Wandless had come to accept over the years. Not ones they liked - who ever could? - but when you stop questioning whether something is wrong, you have accepted it.

The moment Dr Collins hinted at the termination, Emilia Harris stopped accepting those truths.

"Because," she began slowly, choosing her words as carefully as Callum had done, "in their warped way, they think it's the best solution. Once a witch has proven she's fertile enough to produce children, they assume she will still have the desire to keep trying for them. That she's purposefully trying to increase the witchkind population, start an uprising. It's all part of the paranoia and fear that keeps the AMSF in a position of such power. That's also why any Carrier must be executed - to discourage others from following their example."

Rory scoffed. "Carrier? That's what they call you if you're pregnant? They really dehumanise you like that, labelling as if you're transmitting a disease?"

"You haven't heard the way they were using it on the news," Callum said. "They've turned the very notion of Wandless having children into a term of fear."

Silence fell between them once again. It was interrupted by a high-pitched beeping. All three frowned, until Rory realised.

"The oven timer," he said. "I don't know about you, but I bloody need to eat. You certainly do," he added with a nod towards Emilia. "That's assuming" - he turned to Callum - "you aren't planning on throwing her out into the night? Handing her over to the English?"

"No." Callum's voice was soft, pensive. "Of course she can stay."

Emilia slumped back into the armchair a couple of hours later, more satisfied than she had felt in a long time. The warmth of the fire grew more welcoming by the minute. Callum, too, threw himself down into an armchair but with less aggression than he would have when they first met. Rory pottered in from the kitchen, his restored cheeriness adding to this comforting atmosphere, and placed a plate of ginger biscuits on the little wooden table next to Emilia.

"I honestly couldn't eat another bite, Rory," Emilia said.

"Sure you can," he cooed. "That's just your wee stomach still getting accustomed to having proper meals. It'll soon realise my feeble attempt at dinner wasn't enough to fill a hole, and you'll be craving these before you know it. Besides, they're good for the bairn."

She chuckled. It felt good. "Feeble attempt? That was the best lamb I've ever had. And those potatoes..."

"It's no good," Callum said without looking round. "He doesn't take compliments, and he's a perfectionist when it comes to cooking. I swear someday he's going to make a meal that just finishes me off."

"Hell of a way to go though, eh?" Rory smiled at him, and turned towards the kitchen.

"Leave the washing up, dear," Callum called after him, stopping him in his tracks. "Do it later. Or better yet, get Emilia to do it. Can't you just mutter a spell and the dishes will be clean?"

There was a fine line between humour and sarcasm in his voice, but the former was the more dominant and evoked another tired chuckle from her.

"I told you, Callum, it doesn't work that way," she said. "We've each got specific gifts, not a general use of magic. Transforming dirty dishes into clean ones is just not a power I've got - believe me, I've tried."

"How come you're so limited? The way people talk about Wandless, especially the English, it's like you can do anything. Any of you."

"Anyone can pick up a paintbrush," Emilia countered. "Doesn't mean everyone can paint a masterpiece."

Callum frowned, his face frozen halfway between confused and impressed. "But you could learn. People do learn to become artists, how to improve their technique."

"There were teachers," Emilia said. "But not anymore. Now, we can only do what we're naturally able to do."

"Right, right," Callum mumbled thoughtfully. "What was it you do again?"

She sighed, trying to remember how she had described it over dinner. "I can... connect to objects and people. I can sense where everything and everyone is around me, even with my eyes closed. And if I concentrate hard enough, I can move them. Or hold them in place. Does that make sense?"

"People? So you could pick me up and make me fly around the room or something?"

"I could, but people are much harder than objects, much heavier."

"Blame Rory's cooking," Callum snorted.

Emilia burst out laughing. It caught her off guard, felt foreign in her throat. When had she last done this? "No, I mean it takes more effort, more power to move a human. It's your... magical weight, I guess."

"Ah, but you *could* do the dishes?" Rory smiled. "You'd just have to go to the kitchen and magically move them into the sink, and make the sponge fly around scrubbing them?"

Her host had a point. It was the very least she could do, given the hospitality they had shown.

"I don't have my wand," she said. "They took it from me. Without it, I wouldn't have enough control. I might break things. But I guess if I concentrate..."

She placed her hands on the soft arms of the chair and attempted to push herself up. Rory's hand clamped down on her shoulder and playfully pushed her back down again.

"I'm pulling your leg, lass," he said. "Sit down and I'll be back in a while."

And off he went. For a few minutes, nobody spoke. The only sounds were the crackling of the fire, the distant clashing of pots and pans, and the contented sighs of Emilia and Callum. She took this time to look around the room, albeit with as little movement as possible. The couple had made an elegant home, perfectly cluttered with ornaments and sentimental knick-knacks. Every wall, every flat surface bore a framed photo of one or both men, occasionally pictured with friends or relatives.

"You have such a beautiful home, Callum," she said, unable to contain her envy.

"Aye. It's not much, but it's ours. And with nothing but farms around us, we only have each other, which is how I like it."

"Never tempted to have kids yourself then?" she asked, unable to stop herself.

Callum sat up and frowned, preparing to speak. But exhaustion and a full stomach visibly overpowered him and he sank back into his chair. "We talked about it," he said. Emilia didn't press him further.

By the time his husband returned, Callum was snoring and Emilia's eyelids felt heavier than ever. Through her blurry vision, she saw Rory throw his arms in the air comically.

"Jeez, would you both go to bed already?" he grinned. "You're making the place look untidy."

Callum snorted awake and waved Rory away with a huff. Emilia smiled and snuggled deeper into the armchair.

"Leave me here, Rory. I'll be perfectly comfortable."

"Maybe," Rory scoffed. "But you'll be a bloody sight comfier in that bed I took the time to make up for you."

She looked up at him, emotion rising up within her like the sumptuous Yorkshire puddings her host had baked. "Rory," she breathed, "you didn't have to..."

"But, nevertheless, I did," he said. "Up the stairs, first door on the right. Leave your clothes outside the door and I'll have them washed and dry by morning - no arguments. Bathroom's on the other side of the landing. Now off with you."

More than anything, she yearned to stay in the armchair and give in to fatigue. But the prospect of a bed, of pillows and a duvet, was a powerful motivation. Emilia's legs and arms strained into hauling the rest of her upright. She tried to thank Rory again, but overpowering gratitude trapped the words in her throat. Her host simply tapped her on the arm in acknowledgement. His kindly smile was almost enough to unleash a flood of weary, happy tears.

In a daze, Emilia climbed the stairs, ignoring the loud creaks or the unintentional knocks she took to the elbow as she navigated the narrow stairwell. Sure enough, a door lay open to the right as she reached the upper floor, the flickering glow of firelight dancing through the gap. The room she entered was cosy and perfect, with rickety furniture arranged around the small open fire to one side and an impossibly inviting bed to the other.

Without even thinking, or listening out to see if Rory and Callum were behind her, Emilia stripped to her underwear and shoved the clothes out onto the landing with her foot, before closing the door behind her. The bed called and she answered.

Despite the radiance of the fire, the thick duvet was crisp and cool but warmth spread throughout the Wandless as she slipped underneath. Her head sank into the pillow but felt lighter than ever, a significant weight taken off her mind.

For the first minute, the bed felt alien and she couldn't understand why. Then her wandering mind realised; this was the first time she had been in a bed since the Sanctuary, the night before last. Even so, that had been a restless night, knowing what the morning's appointment with Dr Collins might bring. Since then, there hadn't been a moment to rest, so to suddenly be enveloped by comfort, to know she was safe to sleep without fear of...

Over the crackling flames, something louder cracked. Emilia's eyes darted for the source of the sound, but it came from outside the cottage. Not daring to leave the safety of the duvet and risk being exposed, she instinctively reached out with her power, probing the darkness beyond the window. Nothing. She scanned a wider range, searching the perimeter of the building and every room within it. Rory and Callum were the only people around, the former gently trying to wake the latter back in the living room. Must have been an animal, perhaps a fox snapping a hollow stick underfoot. She probed again just to be sure, and was certain they were alone.

No. There was another presence. Something new. Something in this very room. She wondered why she had never noticed it, but realised this was the first time she had used her power at this angle, her body laid out before her.

There, beneath her abdomen, so faint she almost couldn't sense it. But it was definitely there, calm and slumbering, roughly the size of a plum.

She strained to get a stronger sense of it, to form a sharper picture in her head, but it remained indistinct. The effort sapped what little energy she had left. She lost all consciousness and fell into the deepest of slumbers.

13

Deep but troubled slumber. Emilia's dreams were a hazy mess of swirling dark clouds and the growl of unseen quad bikes. Flashes of the Sanctuary appeared, the geography warped by her sleeping mind, the streets of her former home packed with shadowy uniformed figures. Eventually, the bikes appeared, speeding towards her, past her, barely missing her.

Memory strived to override fear, guiding her as she fled, but her legs felt sluggish. Terror retook control as she arrived at the outer fence - the escape route she had taken no longer existed. She scoured the barrier in either direction, but it was taller than she remembered, the barbs sharper, and the shadows drew closer and closer. Suddenly, Emilia found herself in a corner but when she tried to double back, a new fence had risen. There was nothing left between the shadows and her. She had to fight. No other choice.

Reaching out with her magic, Emilia pushed them away. She only wanted to discourage them from approaching but the shadows were hurled backwards, lighter than humans ever could be, like leaves swept away in a gale. Each one crashed into the second fence - visibly made of wire, yet the collision gave the impression of concrete. The spine-chilling crunch of bones, the squelching explosion of organs, and the short but shrill screams of death echoed into the void, deafening her. And still they came, more and more. She fought to control her panicked breathing, she had to fight on. One shadow got closer and closer, reaching for her shoulder.

"Emilia," it called, physically shaking her.

She woke up screaming. The hand was still on her. She threw them off, both physically wrenching the hand away from her shoulder and magically thrusting them backwards. Rory grunted in pain.

Slowly the room came into focus, along with realisation. The older man stood and rubbed his back, wincing from the awkward angle at which he had hit the chest of drawers.

"Rory. I'm so sorry. I didn't mean..."

He held up a hand, cutting her off. It was almost as if he had his own powers, but she knew it was just the commanding, comforting presence he brought to the room.

"Not your fault," he grunted. "Well, it is, but you didn’t mean it. I just wanted to come check on you. Could hear you thrashing about in bed, and then... well, I'm guessing I wasn't the only thing in here that suffered from your nightmares."

He gestured to the rest of the room. Scattered around the floor were all the furnishings that previously made these four walls so homely. Any photo frames or ornaments now lay on the carpet, most shattered. The guest toiletries that were atop the white chest of drawers were beneath the window on the opposite side of the room, the unit itself askew and partially blocking the doorway. The wicker chair next to it was now upside down and in the corner. The curtains had been half flung open. The more Emilia looked around, the more she realised nothing was in its original position, as if a cyclone had redistributed the detritus around the room. All except the bed where she lay. The eye of the storm.

She turned to Rory, a question forming on her trembling lips. He shook his head.

"Fear not," he smiled. "Callum and I are both fine. Well, he's a little shaken but neither of us are injured. Looks like it was all contained here."

"I'm so, so sorry," she repeated. "I've only had my powers back for a day. The woman on the news said I might..."

Emilia came to a decision she hadn't even known she was debating, and she threw back the covers, not bothering to cover her near nakedness, eyes searching for her clothes.

"And where do you think you're going?"

"Away from here. Where are my...?"

"Already washed, and drying as we speak. Just as I promised."

Emilia glared at him. "Well, then, do either of you have clothes I can borrow? Doesn't matter if they don't fit, I just need to get away. I really appreciate you helping me, I do, but I don't want to hurt either of you and..."

"Get back into bed," Rory commanded, suddenly gripping her just below the shoulders and almost carrying her back towards the duvet. Emilia was surprised by his strength, and too emotionally wrecked to fight back. "Sit tight, and I'll go get some herbal tea. I heard that's good for calming the body - not sure if it'll work on one as dangerous as yours, but it's worth a try."

"No, Rory, really... I should..."

"You should take a moment to calm down. You're not traversing the Highlands in your knickers. Just sit tight and I'll be back in a mo."

"I..." she began, but she lacked the energy to argue.

"Thanks."

He smiled and ducked out of the bedroom, closing the door gently behind him.

Emilia heard his weathered old feet thumping down the stairs, the occasional groan as his injury from the chest of drawers flared up. She quickly reached out with her power, concentrating on her own body. The plum-sized presence was still there, quivering. Emilia controlled her breathing, focusing on the life growing within her, and gradually they calmed down.

Her relief was interrupted by another set of footsteps outside, lighter yet more determined. A shadow slid past the slit in the door frame and the second figure stomped downstairs.

"What on earth are you doing?" she heard Callum demand through the thin, old floors of the cottage. There was a pause as Rory ignored him, and when Callum next spoke, his voice came from further away, roughly where the kitchen was.

"You're making her tea? You should be throwing her out - with or without clothes. Why are you still helping her?"

"She was just having a nightmare," Rory said. "If she can get a good night's sleep, she'll be right as rain."

"No, she won't. You don't just sleep off being a witch. Or a killer."

"That was self-defence."

"So she says."

There was a sudden slam, perhaps a palm against a door or worktop. "Oh come off it, dear. You've spent time with her, you've talked to her. Does she seem dangerous to you?"

"Yes, frankly. When you and I have a nightmare, it doesn't wreck the place. What if she'd torn off a door? Thrown something out of a window? What if she'd messed around with all the furniture in our room? We could have been crushed to death."

"Now you're just being ridiculous."

"Am I? She said it herself over dinner: she's not really sure what she's capable of. And she's already killed four people."

"Four soldiers who were trying to kill her first. Trying to take her back to that godforsaken Sanctuary."

"You ever think there's a reason the English put all their witchkind in those Sanctuaries? Maybe there's just too many dangerous ones down there."

"I don't care," Rory said, another slam to emphasise his point. "Witches and wizards are people. She is a person. She's scared, and lost, and just trying to..."

"Just trying to what? Even if she gets to Edinburgh, what's she going to do then? Hide in a cupboard for a few years until it's safe to come out?"

There was a pause, and when Callum spoke again he was forcibly composed, his words quieter. Emilia strained to hear what he said, despite desperately wishing she could block the entire conversation out.

"The English witch hunters are already lining up at the border, begging the Prime Minister to let them in. And I reckon he'll let them. Our Wandless are under strict surveillance, but there's rumours of groups seeking to overthrow him so they can use their powers as they damn well please. The PM already announced he's got Abertay University working on our own version of that containment field or whatever it is they use, and from what I heard, they're getting damn close. And cooperating with the English to find this rogue witch will remind ours what'll happen if they step out of line. It'll remind them they should be thankful they've still got their freedom in Scotland."

"What's your point, Callum?"

"My point, dear," Callum said, his restraint oozing through the rickety floors, "is that neither the English nor our own government are going to take kindly to our aiding and abetting the most wanted woman in Britain. Did you ever think of that?"

"Of course, I did but..."

"Letting her stay, cooking her dinner, washing her clothes - that's all bad enough. But taking her to the capital? No, I won't allow it."

"You won't allow it?" Rory scoffed. "Since when do you allow me to do anything? I'm my own man, husband of mine."

"I'm serious, Rory. Don't take that woman to the city. As soon as her clothes are dry, we're kicking her out."

"No," Rory roared, a third slam on the kitchen side. This one was followed by a shattering sound - too heavy to be a glass, likely a mug. "*I* won't allow *that*."

Silence hung in the air. Through her power, Emilia could feel rather than see the standoff in the kitchen, each man staring his partner down. She braced herself for Callum's retort, and was surprised to hear Rory speak first.

"I was raised to believe the best thing you can do in life is to help someone unable to help themselves. Y'know what - screw how I was raised. That is what I believe. And I've tried to do that in whatever way I can. Bigger tips for flustered waitresses. Change, when I have it, for the homeless. Our regular clean outs and trips to charity shops. But I'm getting old, and I still feel like I haven't made a difference. But with Emilia...? This is the closest I'll ever come to doing something important."

"Rory, you don't know..."

"No, Callum, I do know. I know the fear I see in that girl's eyes is the real deal. I know her story, the situation she's in is real, too - because why would anyone tell a lie so big, just to stay in a random little cottage in the middle of nowhere? I know that if I hadn't stopped her leaving just now, she'd be stumbling through the fields in the freezing night as we speak. I know that if we get her to where she's going, she's going to be alright. I know if we don't, if we let her try to make the journey herself, she's dead. She and the bairn."

He let this hang in the air for a moment. Only then did Emilia become aware of the tears rolling down her face.

"And I know," Rory finished, "I'm not going to be able to live with myself if that happens."

More silence, broken by the occasional tinkling as he gathered up the broken crockery.

"Rory, I'm sorry," Callum eventually said. "I know you mean well, I know you see the good in people - it's one of the many reasons I love you, you great numpty. It just scares me so much... the thought that someone can have such power, what they can do with it."

"She's not like that. She..."

"I know. I know she's not. She's a sweet girl, you can tell that. But she is still dangerous. And the people who are after her even more so. This isn't our fight."

"It's everyone's fight. Witchkind aren't all that different to us - they might be able to do stuff we can't, but they're still normal people. They still get scared. They still need help."

"But..."

"What if I were a wizard? Would you help me? Would you still love me?"

Callum didn't answer at first. Emilia wished she could see his face but the defeat in his voice told her everything.

"Of course I would," he said. "You'd still be you."

"Exactly," Rory says. "And she's Emilia, this sweet, lost

girl who needs our help. So you're going to hand me a mug from that cupboard over there, you're going to go back to bed while I make her tea, and in the morning, we're going to take her to where she wants to go."

She heard soft footsteps and clattering as Callum did as he was bid, then made his way out of the kitchen.

"And Callum, dear," Rory called after him, "I know you're just trying to protect me. It's one of the many reasons I love you."

14

There was an urgent knocking at the door. Whoever was on the other side pounded away with a rhythm of four, occasionally shouting her name.

"Miss Anderson," the woman barked. "Miss Anderson, please open up."

The cacophony of wooden thuds and aggressive outburts enabled Lucy to get up from the sofa and tiptoe to the door without being heard. She peered through the peephole and squinted at her midnight visitor.

The woman wore some sort of military uniform, but certainly not a DRS one. The rigid cap on her head combined with the stripes on her lapels and commanding attitude suggested she was an officer. Her facial features were as harsh as her voice, and this clearly wasn't just the distorted effect of the peephole. There seemed to be someone else in the hallway, at least one other person, but just out of sight.

"Miss Anderson," the officer called. "If you don't open up now, I'll..."

"Can I help you?" Lucy called back through the door.

"Miss Anderson, open the door please."

"Who are you?" she asked. "What do you want?"

"Captain Amanda Hawthorne of the Anti-Magic

Security Force," the officer replied in a terse and rehearsed manner. "We have a few questions. We're here with the authority and support of the Scottish Army, so if you don't allow us inside, you'll be obstructing a military investigation."

"We *are* working with the English, Miss Anderson," a Scottish man said with a softer voice. "Please allow us a few moments and we'll leave you in peace."

Lucy cautiously unlocked the door and jumped back as the captain barged into her apartment. She was followed by a younger man in the same uniform, and then the Scottish officer with a trim moustache and an apologetic look upon his face.

"Good evening, Miss Anderson," he said. "I am Colonel Reid. We're assisting the English in their investigation - I'm sure you've heard all about it on the news. Captain Hawthorne here requested to meet with you. As a DRS citizen, you are of course under no obligation to answer her questions..."

"But -" the captain scowled.

"But," Reid finished, "your co-operation will be greatly appreciated."

Lucy looked between the colonel and the captain and weighed her options for a brief moment. She closed the door and gestured to the lounge area. "Please, take a seat."

"I'd prefer to stand, Miss Anderson," Hawthorne replied, audibly struggling to keep a civil tone. "I'll come straight to the point. When was the last time you heard from Emilia Harris?"

A chill ran through Lucy's entire body. As soon as the knocking had begun, she'd known this would be about Emilia, but to hear her name used so directly...

"The escaped witch?"

"Don't play dumb with me," the captain sneered. "You

must have seen the news. In fact, isn't that what you were watching as we came in?"

She jerked her head towards the large television at the other end of the lounge area, a smug smile spreading across her lips. Lucy swallowed. Sure enough, a news desk could be seen on the screen. The figures around it were discussing rumours of a Scottish-English alliance in the hunt for the Carrier - rumours Lucy now knew could be firmly laid to rest.

She had been watching the news all day, ever since flicking it on this morning as part of her breakfast routine and seeing the image of Emilia. Lucy had called in sick and barely left the sofa as she waited for word on what became of the Wandless woman.

Of course, it was almost certainly a bad idea to admit that but clearly little got past this shrewd English captain. An element of honesty would most likely keep Lucy out of trouble - not that she had done anything wrong - and yet, she felt compelled to lie to this brash woman. Besides, how much could she really know?

"Of course, Captain," she said. "I'm still a little confused by this visit. Yes, I was watching earlier when I got home from work, but I fell asleep on the sofa. I only woke up when you knocked."

The blanket she had wrapped around her for comfort while she watched, now casually strewn across the sofa, supported her story.

"You haven't answered my question. When did you last talk to Harris?"

The arrogant glare in the captain's eyes fuelled Lucy's defiance and she met the officer's gaze with equal determination.

"Nine years ago," she said. "Before you lot had her arrested."

The captain bristled. "She was at the centre of a catastrophic terrorist attack."

"As were dozens of other innocent protestors."

Hawthorne advanced on Lucy, until their faces were just an inch away from each other. "Where is she?"

Lucy stood her ground. "I don't know."

"You mean to tell me you haven't heard from her for almost a decade when you used to meet every six months?"

A wry smile hid Lucy's surprise at how much the captain knew. There would be no point in lying about everything, but she wasn't about to make it easy for this woman to get whatever it was she wanted. Not if Emilia was in danger.

"What do you expect me to say? I've got a direct line into the concentration camp you locked her away in, and..."

"Don't get smart with me, Miss Anderson, or I'll..."

The colonel stepped in and held Hawthorne by the elbow. The captain flinched and for a moment Lucy thought she would turn around and punch him, but she managed to restrain herself.

"Captain," the colonel said, "need I remind you this was to be a civil enquiry and you were not to harass Scottish civilians."

Hawthorne glared at him, then turned back to Lucy, taking a few steps back. "Fine. Miss Anderson, we believe Harris is making her way here. She was last seen in a town just south of the border and the car she stole was found close to the River Tweed, where she almost certainly crossed into Scotland."

"Scotland's a big place, Captain. What makes you think she's heading here?"

Hawthorne rolled her eyes dramatically. "You're her sister."

Lucy's heart plummeted. So they did know. Despite

how much effort her father had gone to keep it from both their mothers, the English military had worked it out.

"Half-sister, actually," was all she could say.

"Regardless," the captain sneered, "You're her only relative north of the border. I've had experts scouring her digital footprint and all links point to you. There's nowhere else she can be going."

"Well, as I said, I haven't heard from her. She might just be heading for the airport - Edinburgh's the only one close to that part of the English border. I've heard..."

"She's coming here," the captain said, and Lucy knew she was right. "And when she gets here, I expect you to inform us immediately. Stall her, keep her here, and we'll come and collect her."

The captain produced a small device from her pocket, a palm sized slab of plastic with a single button, and thrust it towards Lucy. "This links directly to the command centre we've set up in the city - the moment she's here, press this button and we'll mobilise."

Lucy reached for the device, but the captain maintained her firm grip. "Fail to do so and you will be guilty of obstructing this investigation, both in your country and mine. The penalty for which is severe - in fact, I will personally ensure it is."

"Captain." The colonel's stern voice made Hawthorne relinquish the device.

"Apologies, Colonel. Just making sure Miss Anderson understands the stakes, given her personal connection to the Carrier. And her... affiliations."

"I don't know what you're-"

"Yes, you do, Miss Anderson," said Hawthorne. Her glare transformed into a polite smile that looked utterly out of place on her severe features. "Thank you for your time and cooperation, Miss Anderson. We'll let you get some rest."

She turned smartly towards the door, barking "Lieutenant" as she did so, and the third man scurried after her as she marched out of the apartment. The colonel waited until she was out in the hallway before presenting Lucy with a small card.

"If you do hear from Miss Harris," he said. "Please call us instead. This is, after all, a Scottish operation, as Captain Hawthorne seems to have forgotten. Apologies for disturbing you."

The colonel lifted his cap slightly and nodded politely, before following the captain out of the apartment. Lucy closed the door behind them and bolted it, then wandered, dazed, back to the sofa. She tossed the card and the beacon on the console table as she sat down.

"...claim they have indeed seen AMSF forces crossing the border and entering Scotland as the witch hunt continues," the newsreader was saying - but Lucy wasn't listening.

Ever since she had learned of Emilia's escape that morning, part of her had wondered if her half-sister would travel here. But the logical part of her brain told her it was too far, too dangerous. She couldn't even begin to conceive how Emilia had made it this far, but she knew the Captain was right.

If Emilia was already across the border, she could well turn up at her door within the next 24 hours - if she didn't get caught, of course.

Lucy stood from the sofa and began to prepare.

15

The drive to Edinburgh was the most uncomfortable Emilia had ever endured. The car itself was fine; in fact, the seats in Rory's family saloon were much softer and warmer than the compact car she had stolen the night before.

"Heated seats," he said as he saw her confused but content expression a short while after they left the cottage. She smiled nervously, and thus his effort to break the tension failed.

They travelled along the A1, the only major road in this area, although few cars were heading in the same direction - no doubt the effect of stricter checks at the Tweedmouth border crossing. To the right, Emilia could make out the harsh expanse of the North Sea beyond flat fields. To the left, hedgerows and embankments hid Scottish farmland from sight. Rory chirpily informed them they were halfway there, to which she responded with a timid "thank you". Callum merely grunted.

Neither of the men had made eye contact since they had first departed, and Callum had barely spoken to Emilia other than to insist she sit up front, taking the back seat for himself - something she could tell had upset Rory. He, of course, concentrated on driving but Emilia caught him stealing a glance at his husband whenever he could. Callum, meanwhile, stared permanently ahead, barely aware of either person in the front seats. Every now and then, Emilia wondered why he even came along, but reminded herself he just wanted to protect his husband from the forces they might encounter. And from her.

The only sound Callum responded to was the telltale growl of a motorbike or some other military vehicle, each of which mercifully rolled past them on the way to the city. The drivers occasionally slowed to check inside cars at random, but sped away when they found nothing. One black AMSF car came up alongside them and Emilia could feel Callum tense up behind her. She feigned sleep, as Rory had suggested before they set out, while he lifted a hand from the steering wheel to wave politely to the driver. They pulled away, and Callum let out an audible sigh of relief.

"See, dear," Rory called back. "We have nothing to worry about."

Callum ignored him. Rory sighed, his breath loaded with more despair than that of his husband and shuffled in his seat as he refocused on the road ahead.

Emilia couldn't contain her guilt any longer.

"I'm so sorry," she said. "I didn't mean to cause trouble or get either of you involved in this. I just needed a place to stay for the night and..."

"If you say I'm sorry one more time, I'm going to drop you by the side of the road and you can walk the rest of the way," Rory said, no hint of aggression or threat in his voice.

"Good. Then I'll be..."

"You're not going anywhere, lass. I said we'd get you to the city, and that's what we're going to do. You'd never make it on your own, even with those fancy powers of yours. Even if you did, you wouldn't be there till tonight and I imagine the authorities will be keeping an eye out for suspicious English women skulking around in the dark."

"But..."

"Emilia, it's fine."

She opened her mouth to speak, but restrained herself. Rory chuckled.

"I can hear how badly you want to say it. Let's talk about something else to take your mind off things, eh? It'd be good to have a little conversation going for the rest of the journey."

Callum clearly disagreed as Emilia heard shuffling behind her. She magically probed to see - or rather, feel - what he was doing, and sensed him fishing in his pocket for something. He pulled out a set of headphones, plugged them into his phone and began tapping on the screen. A tinny rendition of classical music blared out of the earbuds, muffled slightly as he tucked them into his ears.

Rory glared at him for a few moments in the rear view mirror, but Callum ignored him. Rory snorted.

"The Wandless problem was never something we could agree on," Rory said. "No offence."

"None taken. Do you often argue about it? I mean..."

"You mean like last night?" Rory said, turning to her with a knowing look. "It's fine, Emilia. We both know how well sound travels through those old floors. You can't hide anything in our home. No, that's the worst we've ever argued about it, but we've had debates that have raged for hours. I'm firmly of the belief that witches are no different to the rest of us, and should be treated as such. Callum wants them all removed from our so-called normal society, or at the very least registered, licenced and constantly monitored."

“Isn’t that what you do up here?”

"Sort of," Rory said. "There's a register of all known witchkind and that flags up when they apply for a job, for example. But it's only for the eyes of the government, the authorities, people in recruitment. Providing they don't use their magic or expose themselves, they're allowed to live normal lives like the rest of us. Callum has never been comfortable with that. Thinks they should all be open about who they are and what they can do so people can choose whether they want to work with witches, live next to witches and so on."

"I see."

It was impossible for Rory to miss the unease in her voice.

"Don't be mistaken, lass," he said, "it's not like he wants any of them deported or executed or anything horrific like that. What you say the English are doing to Wandless mothers-to-be is a far cry from anything he'd ever want."

"Good to know," was all Emilia could bring herself to say.

The urge to throw the door open and hurl herself out of the car intensified. If Callum didn't trust the Wandless, he didn't trust her - so could she even trust him? He might hand her over to the Scottish Army or AMSF when they reached the city. She hadn't had the chance to check the news, so for all she knew, there might be a reward for assistance with her capture. Yes, Rory might support her, but what could one kindly man do against the authorities and his own husband? The previously comfortable car was now a cage on wheels, speeding her back to the hands of witch hunters.

Another AMSF motorbike sped past, and Callum gave no reaction. If he wanted her arrested, why would he wait until they reached Edinburgh? It would be easy enough to alert the passing soldiers. The tension gripping Emilia's body loosened, but she was still far from relaxed.

Rory cleared his throat, a blatant move to clear the air. "Are you looking forward to becoming a mum?" he asked. "Was it something you planned before...?"

"Before I was arrested?" The driver winced at the bitterness in her tone. Emilia sighed. "I... I don't know. It's something I always assumed I would do, when I was older and married or in the right relationship. It was this distant milestone somewhere in my future - I'd get there as and when. But when they took me to the Sanctuary, that future disappeared. Even now, I can only think as far as getting to the city. Beyond that, I don't know what's going to happen, so why...?" She trailed off.

"Why get your hopes up?" Rory finished. "Emilia, I'm so sorry."

The fugitive forced herself to chuckle. "I thought that word was forbidden."

"Right you are," Rory replied.

Hills and hedges rolled past for a minute as Emilia sought a way to divert the conversation.

"Did you and Callum ever want to become parents?"

"Oh," he said, not taking his eyes off the road, "that went out the window years ago. Callum and I discussed it for years. But... I don't know..."

"Rory, if you don't want to talk about it..."

"I'm fine talking about it," Rory replied, shooting her a gentle smile. "What's done is done. Or not done, in this case."

"Honestly, I didn't mean to intrude. It was just a..."

"It's fine. Might be good to talk about it. It's a bit of a sore subject with him, and as you saw from our home in the middle of nowhere, we're not exactly surrounded by neighbours I can talk to."

Rory inhaled, bracing himself. "I was very much in

favour, Callum wasn't so sure. He had so many worries: what if he had to work late, and I was left handling the bairn on my own? What if they got sick or injured, and we couldn't get them to a hospital in time? What if the English invaded, and we're pretty much on the front line? It got a little silly, almost funny at points. We had a good laugh about that English one.

"Eventually, I worked out he was just scared he wouldn't be good enough as a dad. His never stuck around, so it's not like he had a role model to base himself on. By the time I brought him round, got him to accept that it'd be a learning curve for both of us, we were too old. I don't think we were even that old - life starts at 40, eh? - but the adoption agencies wouldn't have it. We went through a period of always having a couple of dogs, and we poured our love on those, but it wasn't the same. And when Mabel passed five years back, we decided to wait a while before getting another animal. I suppose we became comfortable just the two of us."

Emilia fought the impulse to utter the forbidden word, but she felt it. From what little she had seen of the two men, there was no doubt in her mind they would have made phenomenal parents: caring, devoted, firm when necessary. Even Callum had shown how protective he would be of his family.

Rory could clearly sense what she was thinking, and turned to smile at her. With so much fear around the Wandless and what they could do, it was easy for Emilia to forget how perceptive ordinary people could be.

"We would have been very happy," he said, "but we still are. And that's all that matters, eh?"

He turned back to face the road, flinching slightly as another motorbike seemingly came out of nowhere, zipping past as it swerved out of a country lane.

"What about family members?" Emilia asked. "Do they not visit? Do you have nieces and nephews you can spoil instead?"

Rory shook his head. "We're both from quite small families, and they're all in the far-flung reaches of Scotland, so we don't get to see each other much. You get used to it."

Emilia sighed. "I know the feeling."

"What about your family?" he asked. "Were they with you in the Sanctuary?"

"I'm the only Wandless in the family. Neither of my parents have powers, and nor did my brother."

"Did?"

"He died at Harwich," Emilia said, her voice breaking. It had been a long time since she had spoken about Ian. "He came along to support me, and..."

She tried to finish the sentence, but failed. Rory nodded in understanding.

"Presumably you're still allowed to contact your parents, though?"

"Sort of. We can send letters or emails, even have phone or video calls, but they're all monitored closely. For security, they say."

"Do they not get to visit?"

"No," she sighed. "Again, it's all about security concerns. They try to keep a distance between us. In fact, witchkind families are separated upon arrest. They're sent to different Sanctuaries."

"What?"

Both Rory and Emilia frowned. This splutter of disgust came from Callum. Neither had noticed him remove his headphones and listen in to their conversation, presumably after catching words over the top of his music.

He leaned forward and rested his hands on the back of

Emilia's seat, craning round to see her face. "But why?" The hostility in his voice was gone, replaced by bewilderment.

"Because they don't want another Harwich," she said. "That started as a democratic protest, but one family managed to rile enough witchkind up to convince them to start fighting. That many Wandless in one place is dangerous enough but... I mean, scientists are still looking into it but apparently witchkind can amplify each other's powers if they're blood-related. Something to do with the... you know what, I can't remember the science behind it. The point is that's what this family did. Ever since the government learned that, they keep all Wandless separate from their relatives. Especially those of us that were involved in Harwich, even if we were just in the protest march."

"But that doesn't necessarily prevent you from conspiring together. Just because you're not related, doesn't mean you won't ally with others in your Sanctuary."

"No, but they make sure they keep us busy," Emilia said. "Too busy to try anything - and we've proven to be very valuable as labour. Each Sanctuary is set up with work centres to do tasks that clearly no human wants to do."

"Like what?"

"All the little things you don't really think about: packing boxes, shelling peanuts, weighing out food or washing powder or stuff like that so it all matches the weight on the packaging. My job was to wind plastic tubing and wires around bobbins so they didn't get tangled."

"That sounds... thrilling."

"It keeps us occupied. If we're working, we're too busy

and too exhausted to organise an uprising or work out how to escape..."

Rory snorted. "That's working out well for them."

"Oh, I'm not the first to break out on my own. I might be the one who has got the furthest - I don't know. If someone breaks out, we never hear what happens to them unless their arrest or... death makes the news. But by keeping us busy, they stop us from attempting mass breakouts. Plus, it's free labour."

"You're not paid for what you do?" Callum asked, his voice rising.

"We get credit. Save it up and we can exchange it for a luxury, like chocolate or decent pillows."

"Disgusting. Those documentaries I watched on the English Sanctuary system suggested life was normal in those villages, that Wandless were free to live and work with one another. I always assumed that included your family and friends. They made it seem to be more like a gated community than a..."

"A prison?" Emilia finished.

“Don’t the people of England know about this?” Callum said. “Can’t they do anything about it?”

“They know,” she said. “They just don’t care. As long as they’re safe from us, that’s all that matters.”

The car fell silent.

16

The uncomfortable silence resumed for the rest of the drive, but it was a different discomfort that deterred anyone from speaking. Callum sat brooding in the back seat, but the tension between him and his husband was gone. Emilia could almost hear his brain whirring, processing what she told him about the Sanctuaries and the government's attitude to Wandless lives.

Even when they made a brief detour into Haddington, a small town just off the main road, the trio did not speak. Rory recovered his friendly demeanour when talking to the old woman who worked in the charity shop they visited. Callum stayed in the car, while Emilia followed Rory and found a change of clothes. The best she could manage was a flowery dress that was one size too large and twenty years out of fashion. It was lighter than her Sanctuary-issued clothing and therefore colder, but it was softer too - and that alone made it the most comfortable thing she had worn for a decade. She also found a long beige coat to keep her warm.

Emilia changed in the public toilets nearby, leaving her old clothes in the cubicle. She would never need them again.

Shortly after they rejoined the A1, the traffic slowed and

soon brought them to a standstill. The silence continued, only now it was because none of them wanted to utter the horrible thoughts they all shared. Callum was the first to break it.

"They're obviously checking every vehicle heading into the city,' he said. "Only reason for tailback this far out - they must be searching everyone thoroughly."

Emilia scanned the horizon ahead. No sign of military vehicles or soldiers, but the line of cars stretched as far as she could see, very occasionally crawling a few feet forward. Her hand drifted towards the door handle.

"I'll go on foot from here," she said. "I don't want you to get you caught up in this."

"Too late for that," Callum scoffed.

"Well, I don't want you to get in trouble. Honestly, you've been so kind and thank you for taking me this far but I -"

"You're not going anywhere," Rory said. "We'll get you through this, I promise."

"But..."

"You'll get us in more trouble if you bail out now," Rory said. "People in all the other cars will wonder why you're wandering off in the middle of all this, and they'll direct the soldiers to us."

"My husband is right," Callum added.

"Thank you, dear."

Emilia reluctantly let go of the handle. "Then what do we do?"

Callum leant forward, squinting at the road ahead. "If memory serves, there's a junction not far ahead. We'll turn off there and find another route."

"Aye, there is," Rory said, straightening up, a curious smile forming in the corner of his mouth. "And I know where it leads. At the risk of sounding stereotypically

Scottish, we'll..." - he grinned as he paused for effect - "… take the low road."

Duddingston Low Road was a narrow lane that wound round the bottom of Holyrood Park, a group of hills just outside the city of Edinburgh. Emilia and her companions were unchallenged as they left the A1, and the two tranquil coastal towns that were less than a mile away from being absorbed by the growing Scottish capital did not react to their presence.

As they travelled along the foot of Arthur's Seat, the tallest hill, the rooftops of Edinburgh came into view. Emilia’s heart soared and her flight from the Sanctuary seemed that much further away. But her optimism deflated as she saw what awaited them.

"Oh dear," Rory said.

"You said they wouldn't be checking a road this minor," Callum growled.

"I thought..."

Emilia’s hand snapped towards the door handle again. Rory caught the movement.

"Don't, Emilia. It'll just draw more attention. And you'll never outrun them on foot."

"Outrun them?" Callum said. "You're not suggesting we...?"

"Look, everybody calm down," Rory barked, an unusual and unfitting tone for him. "If we're calm and civil, maybe we can get through this. Emilia, pretend you're asleep and follow my lead."

The witch shuffled into position, turning towards her driver and hunching. "Are you sure this will work?"

"No," said Rory.

Even after she closed her eyes, she could see them. With her magic, she could feel them.

Two motorbikes, each with an AMSF soldier aboard.

One military all-terrain vehicle, bearing the proud blue and white cross of the Scottish Army, with two soldiers on the road and two in the front seats, poised for anyone attempting a quick getaway. No official cordon or any physical barrier but the road was too small for anyone to pass without this group's permission.

Her stomach twisted. It was a smaller force than she had dealt with on the night of her escape, but far more threatening. The Scots were renowned for their marksmanship, a crucial factor in them winning the Separation War. More importantly, if they were co-operating with the English, that meant there would be a lot more AMSF troops in the area. If they could spare two bikes for this back route into the city, who knew how many there would be guarding the main roads, or patrolling the streets. And all of them just a radio call away.

Since leaving the Sanctuary, all she had thought about was herself and her destination, but now Emilia was increasingly conscious of Rory and Callum. Just yesterday, they had been a kindly couple living a quiet life in their remote cottage, but within the next few moments they would be branded criminals, harbouring a fugitive. Rory was right, she couldn't outrun these soldiers but nor could he and his husband. All she had wanted was shelter for the night, and now she had ruined two innocent lives.

Rory must have been able to sense her distress with that innate human perception that witchkind tended to lose or ignore, because he turned towards her.

"Don't panic, Emilia," he said, doing a remarkable job of sounding calm. "You too, Callum. Trust me, we'll be fine. Nobody do anything rash."

Emilia curled up under her coat, but it had little to do with the pretence of sleep - the tension made it impossible to relax in her seat. She felt the soldiers getting closer as

Rory slowed the car and rolled towards them, winding down the window as they drew near.

"Afternoon, gents," Rory said with practised charm. "What's all this about?"

"Rogue Wandless from England," a gruff Scottish voice replied from just outside Rory's window. "These boys are convinced she's heading for the city, so we're helping them check every vehicle that's heading here. What business have you got in Edinburgh today, sir?"

"A Wandless, eh? Is she dangerous?"

"Have you not been watching the news? She's already killed four of the English witch hunters."

Rory leant on the window, capitalising on the relaxed attitude of this soldier. Perhaps the man felt his posting on this lesser-used route into the city meant he was less likely to encounter the fugitive. Maybe his relaxed attitude could work in their favour - by Rory's friendly demeanour, Emilia guessed he was hoping for the same.

"Yeah, but at the risk of sounding disrespectful," Rory began, lowering his voice so the AMSF couldn't hear, "that's the English. Does she really pose a danger to us Scots? What makes them think she's heading to Edinburgh?"

"Not something they're willing to share at the moment. Maybe they think she's heading for the airport, hop a flight to the continent so she can disappear. Doesn't matter - both us and the English have enough troops across the city to stop her from getting that far. So, what business do you have in Edinburgh today, sir?"

Rory shrugged. "Just popping in for the day. Browse some shops, have a meal, maybe take a stroll around the castle. Nothing fancy."

"Might be worth reconsidering your trip given everything that's going on today, sir," the soldier replied.

"And who is travelling with you?"

Emilia sensed him bending down to peer into the car. She had no way to know for sure where he was looking, but could feel his gaze burning through her coat.

"Just my husband in the back there," Rory said, "and my niece here."

"Is there a reason she's hiding under her coat?" the soldier asked, his relaxed tone instantly replaced by suspicion. Emilia could almost hear his brow furrowing.

"A little too much whiskey last night," Rory replied quickly. "Part of why we're going into town - bit of fresh air, some decent food to soak up the alcohol. Maybe a little hair of the dog, eh?"

"Can you wake her up for me, sir?"

Rory stiffened. "Ah, now, have a heart. She's really suffering - self-inflicted, I know, but she just needs to sleep it off for a bit."

"Sorry, sir, but we really do need to check everyone."

"Alright," Rory said. Emilia could feel Callum tense in the back seat as the soldier walked slowly around to her side of the car. As he did, Rory gently pulled the coat away from her and they both made a good show of her waking up.

"We there already, uncle Ror'?" Emilia groaned.

"Almost, sweetheart," he replied, pressing the button to lower the window on her side.

"She's English?" the soldier remarked. Emilia squinted at him sleepily as if surprised he was there. The suspicious frown on his face sent a surge of fear down her spine.

"Aye. Got quite a few relatives on the other side of the border. Big family."

But Rory no longer held the soldier's attention.

"What's your name, madam?" he asked, leaning down to get a closer look at Emilia.

"Sophie. Sophie Robertson."

"Do you have any ID on you? Anything to prove that?"

She made a display of patting around her pockets, then turned to her 'uncle'. "Did I leave my purse at yours?"

"You must have done - probably to make sure I'm buying," Rory replied.

Callum leaned forward. "Yeah, I think I last saw it on the red armchair." Despite all the tension, Emilia felt a surge of comfort and gratitude as Rory's husband weighed in to support their elaborate farce of a ruse.

"Hmm," the soldier mused. "Stay in the car for now. I'm going to have to consult with my colleagues."

They watched in silence as the man walked away, his fellow soldier taking up his previous position by Rory's door. The two men on the motorbikes straightened at the sight of their Scottish ally approaching. The three of them were too far away for Emilia to hear, but she knew how their conversation would go.

Sure enough, one of the bike soldiers dropped from his vehicle and followed the Scottish soldier back to the car. The soldier pointed directly at her, and she saw the AMSF soldier frown under his helmet. He rounded the car and glared at her.

"What d'you say your name was, madam?"

For a second, Emilia panicked, unable to remember the alias she gave barely a minute ago. But, just as the soldier reached for his radio, it came flooding back to her.

"Sophie Robertson. I'm so sorry, I left my ID at my uncle's."

"So I hear," the soldier replied, his voice riddled with suspicion. He pulled a phone from his pocket and tapped in a few commands. In the reflection of the raised, tinted visor on his helmet, Emilia watched as a distorted image of her, the file photo from the Sanctuary, came up on the device. The soldier looked back at her and squinted.

"You're all coming with us," he said. "Remain in the vehicle. You will be escorted to our command centre for questioning." His head snapped up to the Scottish soldiers and barked at them. "One of you take over from the driver. Follow me back to command."

He stomped away towards his motorbike while the soldier who first stopped them pointed at the vehicle, then at his colleague, who started walking lazily towards it.

Callum could contain himself no longer. "Well, this is great. We're screwed. So much for your quiet route in, Rory. What do we do now?"

"I... I don't know," his husband replied.

"We never should have come here. Hand her over, let's just go home."

"Callum, we can't do that. It's too late. We're involved now."

"And whose fault is that?"

The anger and the truth of their words penetrated Emilia, dissolving her fear. She knew what she had to do. She closed her eyes and concentrated.

"Rory, get ready to move."

"Emilia, no," he started, but her arms were already raised, fingers bent into a tense claw as she channelled her power.

Just as the AMSF soldier reached his bike, she yanked it away from him with a flick of the wrist, slamming it into the other bike. The second soldier clung on as his vehicle was thrown against a tree, and before he could jump clear she picked up the first bike with her power and smashed the two together.

Mercifully, Rory took this as his cue and the car lurched forward, knocking the approaching Scottish guard to the ground. He barrelled through the space where the motorbikes once were, swerving around the Scottish Army jeep. The driver glared at them as they passed, frantically firing up his vehicle and attempting a 180-degree turn to follow them.

Callum swore at both Emilia and his husband from the back seat but they were too focused to notice or care: Rory on driving, the Wandless on sensing and stalling their pursuers. Rory wrenched at the wheel and they narrowly avoided mounting a roundabout. He took the first exit and accelerated again, replacing their countryside surroundings with stone houses, innocent and confused bystanders, and busier streets.

They had entered Edinburgh, their destination, but the journey was far from over.

17

The command centre was abuzz with activity, but to Hawthorne it was silent. Devoid of any news regarding the Carrier.

The lieutenant stood by her side, scouring the map that lay on the fold-up table that stood before them in the centre of the marquee. The heat from computers, generators and other military equipment combined with the heavy canvas added humidity to the tense atmosphere.

The tablet on the table before them painted a clear picture of the operation thus far. A map filled the screen, tracking each unit the AMSF and Scottish Army had in the area. As Hawthorne surveyed the map, she saw their checkpoints were in place at every major entry route into the city and even most of the minor ones. They hadn't been allowed to bring enough troops across the border to cover every footpath and minor road, but the motorbikes patrolling both the ring road and the city centre were searching Edinburgh with vigilance. Most of her troops were on bikes - it meant they would be able to weave through traffic and travel faster without fear of the obstacles that would block a car or jeep's passage.

Her superiors had questioned concentrating all their forces on a single city, suggesting it left the motorways free for the Wandless to travel to Glasgow or one of the cities further north. But Hawthorne had remained adamant that Harris was trying to rendezvous with Anderson - who, unsurprisingly, had not contacted them with any further information.

Hawthorne did not expect to hear from Anderson, but the tracking beacon in the device she had given her would alert the captain if she tried to leave the city - most likely with the Carrier. The beacon was also present on the map, represented by a blue circle.

A comms operator called the lieutenant over and the officer moved across the tent. When he returned, his face was not one of optimism.

"Still no sign of the Carrier, Captain," he said. "And the southern checkpoints are requesting further instructions. The traffic is easing up as word spreads of our search - I believe there has even been a news broadcast advising everyone to avoid travelling into Edinburgh. Surely the less traffic there is on the road, the less likely the Wandless is to travel that way? She'll be spotted too easily."

"Everyone maintains their position," the Captain barked, without looking up from the map. "We're not going home until we have that witch in cuffs. Or a bag."

"Understood," the lieutenant said, and walked back over to the comms officer.

Hawthorne was aware of movement to the far right and heard footsteps approaching.

"Captain Hawthorne," Colonel Reid's voice accompanied them. "I'm getting reports from my men that your troops are harassing Scottish citizens at your checkpoints. Need I remind you that the terms of this temporary alliance state that our people will be treated with respect at all times. Bad enough your bikes are buzzing around the city causing a panic. Either you conduct your search in an orderly fashion, or you take your forces back south."

"Thank you, Colonel," she said, still not taking her eyes off the map. "I'm well aware of the terms, having negotiated them mysel..."

She stopped, suddenly aware of urgency in the voice of one of the comms officers. She turned to see a bald man clutching his head-mounted microphone in one hand, pulling it closer to his mouth, and pushing his headphones against his ear with the other.

"...have her in custody? I repeat, do you have her in custody?"

Hawthorne marched over, ignoring protestations from the colonel. She placed a firm hand on the officer's shoulder.

"What's happening?"

The officer raised a hand, gesturing for her to wait. "Backup is en route, I say again, backup is en route. Keep calling out her position."

Hawthorne looked around the cluttered desks of the command centre and snatched a spare headset from under a pile of wires. As she put it on and adjusted the frequency, the bald man spoke.

"Carrier's been spotted at the Holyrood entrance to the city and has fled the scene," the officer said. "She's in a car with two Scottish men, and using her powers against our men in an aggressive manner. Officers are in pursuit but need backup."

"They'll get it," Hawthorne replied, before barking into the mic. "All units, I repeat all units, converge on the city centre. Suspect is on the move from Holyrood Park. Abandon your checkpoints and follow your comms officers' instructions. This needs to be a coordinated effort people - she is not getting away."

The captain marched back to her map, watching the markers lurch across the screen.

"Colonel, she's been spotted," she said, as if he were nothing more than another soldier under her command. "Have your comms team sync with mine, I want all available vehicles and personnel to join in cutting her off, herd her into a corner. Lieutenant, you're with me. Comms, we need eyes in the sky for this one. Come on, people, let's not mess this up."

And with that, she stormed out of the marquee.

18

The engine screamed as Rory pushed the car faster than anyone expected. Every now and then it juddered as he fumbled another gear change, but he quickly learned to recover from these stutters. Behind them, sirens and screeching tyres fuelled their flight.

They careened down a main road towards Edinburgh city centre, buses and cars swerving to avoid them, pedestrians watching in shock and horror. What little Emilia remembered of the city was gone in the panic of the chase. The only familiar landmark was the castle silently looking down on them from its hilltop, glimpsed only briefly down streets and between taller buildings. Rory knew the city well, and that knowledge showed as they swerved unexpectedly down a road or alleyway that led to new areas, but the soldiers in pursuit always seemed one step ahead. Whenever they emerged from another of Rory's shortcuts, a combination of jeeps, cars and motorbikes were waiting for them, both AMSF troops and those of the Scottish Army.

Emilia's blood burned with the magical strain of throwing each one off their trail. Unlike the roadblock and outside the Sanctuary, she couldn't just hurl them away - there were innocent people on the streets, other drivers on the road, and finding a place to safely slam the vehicles took concentration and as fast a reaction as she could muster. Worse still was the effort of disabling and diverting the hefty military vehicles of the Scottish Army, a far greater strain on her powers than the lighter motorbikes and cars. Physical weight was said to make no difference to the more powerful witchkind, but Emilia was out of practice and under pressure.

Fortunately, the Scottish vehicles tended to be less aggressive, merely trying to keep them in sight rather than trying to run them off the road. In any encounter with both English and Scottish forces, it was Emilia's countrymen who took the lead. On one occasion, an AMSF driver nearly smashed into a Scottish jeep as he attempted a high-speed overtake.

She rapidly lost count of how many bikes and cars she threw into walls, lamp posts and bollards. She knew she had ripped at least five engines out from under bonnets. The entire AMSF and DRS forces searching the surrounding areas must have been called in to join the chase - a terrifying thought that Emilia shoved aside as violently as she did the next bikes. If she let that sink in, despair would shatter her strength.

Callum wasn't helping.

"What are you doing?" he bellowed. "We're never going to outrun them. Stop. Surely we can reason with them or something?"

He yelped as Emilia pulled a lone Scottish soldier from his vehicle and dropped him roughly on the roof of a bus stop, the jeep he was driving swerving into a post box.

"Emilia, stop it! What's your plan when you're finished killing all these soldiers?"

"If you'll.. urgh.. notice," Emilia groaned as she spun a motorbike around so that it sped off in the opposite direction, "I'm doing my best... errrargh... *not* to kill anyone."

"Leave her alone, Callum," Rory called, taking them down another side road. "She's tried time and again to leave us out of this. This is my fault. You can have a go at me when we're out of this. Until then, shut up - unless you have anything useful to say."

"When we're out of this? What makes you think -"

"Callum!"

Callum fell silent.

Nothing followed them down the next residential street, so Emilia took a moment to gather her strength and catch her breath. A moment all too brief; three motorbikes growled as they emerged from turnings behind them. She grunted as she crushed all three together, but a black jeep smashed through the wreckage, hot on their tail.

"They're everywhere," Rory shouted. "How are they cutting us off so quickly?"

"Rory," Callum began.

"Callum, if you complain..."

"No, there's a helicopter above us. I only just noticed it. Must be calling out our position to the other troops."

Emilia leaned out of the window and looked up. Sure enough, there was something hovering dozens of metres above them, hanging in the air like a kestrel tracking its prey.

"Emilia," Rory said, "can you...?"

"Already trying."

The helicopter was further away than she had ever had to reach, even before all those years under the influence of the suppression field. She stretched out for it, trying to gain a magical grasp on the skids beneath, the pilot, the crew inside, anything. It was just beyond the reach of her powers, no matter how far she extended them. She could feel them, both the helicopter and its pilot, just not enough to secure a firm hold.

Her concentration was thrown momentarily as Rory pulled the car into a sharp bend. She glanced around. He was using a wide crossroads to turn around and head back the way they had come from, much to the confusion and annoyance of all other motorists. The jeep chasing them was also unprepared for this and roared off down a different road. The driver attempted a turn as sharp as Rory's, but his vehicle was neither small nor agile enough and the road was too narrow. He slammed into a wall with a satisfying crunch, this one without the Wandless' help.

The helicopter banked sharply to follow them, and in doing so the pilot dipped lower. Not by much, but enough for Emilia to wrap her mystic fingertips around the skids. She prodded and from far below she could see the aircraft wobble. She pushed harder, trying to knock it off course, but it continued to follow them. She tried harder still but her more violent shove, exacerbated by the lack of a wand to focus her power, sent it into a corkscrew. She and Callum both gasped as he watched the helicopter hurtle down.

The aircraft was moving faster than anything Emilia had dealt with before but she frantically reached out with her powers, trying to grab it. Once, twice, three times she slowed its descent but it slipped free from her control. Yet as it drew closer to the ground, her grasp grew stronger. On the fourth try, she managed to stop the helicopter's descent, seconds before it crashed into the road. Rory was still speeding ahead so her magical grip began to weaken with distance but she still had enough strength to lower the helicopter gently to the tarmac, blocking the road for the two jeeps that were following them. Just before the aircraft was out of range, she twisted her hands and turned to see the rotors bend and, in one case, snap off.

Emilia faced forwards once more and fought the urge to relax. Preventing the helicopter crash had taken much of what little energy she had left, but the appearance of three Scottish jeeps blocking the left fork in the road ahead forced her to stay alert.

Rory swerved down the right fork, and the jeeps followed, maintaining their rigid formation that blocked the width of the road. Motorbikes at two exits of the next crossroads forced him left, then joined the pursuit. Emilia flicked the drivers from each, the bikes falling down and grinding to a halt.

"Something's not right," Rory said, as much to himself as to the others.

At first, Emilia wasn't sure what he meant. Then she realised.

Tall buildings surrounded them, centuries-old stone gliding past their windows, mostly shops and restaurants. Every now and then, a gap between them showed the castle towering over them. They were in the city centre... and yet there were no other cars around. The road ahead of them was empty, the one behind still blocked by the trio of jeeps, following more than pursuing. Jeeps and bikes emerged from each side road, but only a few swerved out behind them.

Callum voiced the thought they all shared. His tone was incredulous, refusing to believe it. "They're herding us."

Rory sighed heavily, his shoulders sagging with defeat. He slowed briefly, but the drop in speed snapped him out of his brief reverie and he floored the accelerator once more. The jeeps behind maintained their predatory speed.

Emilia's eyes darted back and forth for a potential exit from the rats' maze the military had built from Edinburgh's city streets, but she found none. There was the occasional pedestrian alleyway, too narrow for a vehicle, but there was no way the three of them could outrun this many soldiers. She toyed with opening the door, leaping from the vehicle and running, drawing the troops away from Rory and Callum, but she lacked the courage. Besides, there was no guarantee the soldiers would leave the two of them alone and she wouldn't be able to protect them if she fled. The couple had been so generous to her, she owed it to them to stay put and throw off every vehicle she could.

The thought gave her renewed strength and she mentally reached out for the vehicles behind them. Three jeeps in a line, flanked by four scattered motorbikes. She tentatively gripped each one with her power.

"Rory," she said, "when you get the chance, turn and go back the way we came."

"Have you not seen how many of them are following us?" Callum cried.

"I can handle them, Callum," she said, surprised at her own confidence. "Please, Rory, trust me. Turn around, and I'll do the rest."

Rory looked at her, unsure, but tightened his grip on the wheel. Without a word of warning, he wrenched it around and they bumped up onto the pavement. The jeeps wobbled, but stayed their course. Rory screeched sharply through a tight circle. One bike nearly smashed into them, but with a flick of her hand, Emilia sent it up and over their roof. A second bike crashed into the front of the car, but Rory's sturdier vehicle batted it aside. It span across the road, and Emilia guided it into the path of a third bike. Metal crumpled as they collided, sparks flying as they ground to a halt. She reached for the fourth bike, but the woman riding it had seen the chaos unfold and held back. She retreated out of Emilia's range but the jeeps were nearly upon them.

"Emilia," Rory called, wide eyes fixed on the approaching trio.

"Just keep going. Trust me."

"We're going to crash."

"Ssh, I'm concentrating."

The Scottish soldiers bearing down upon them wore a mix of determination and panic on their faces. Emilia focused. Rory started to slow, but she yelled at him to speed up. She slid her magical force under the three jeeps, hands held out in front of her to channel it, and braced herself. Seconds before the vehicles collided, she jerked her hands upwards and flipped the three jeeps into the air, grunting with mental exertion. Callum gasped and the car veered to the side as Rory gawked in amazement at the three hefty black military transports soaring above them. A bump against the kerb forced him to concentrate on the road once more, but he smiled slightly as he heard the crash of metal falling to the ground.

The road ahead was clear.

"Let's get out of the city," Callum said. "Back home."

"I agree," Emilia sighed, out of breath. "You can drop me somewhere, anywhere on the way and I'll find my own way on foot."

"No, you'll..."

"Rory, please," she said, placing a hand on his arm. "You two have already done so much for me, I can't put you in danger like this anymore. I'll be fine, I'll..."

"Rory, look out!"

Emilia's eyes snapped to the road ahead at the sound of Callum's cry. Four more jeeps had appeared, two from each exit of the roundabout they were approaching. They screeched to a halt, blocking their path. Emilia glanced over her shoulder. The wreckage of the three she had just destroyed blocked that direction. A side road to the left was the only option.

Rory swerved towards it but struggled with the gears as the road shifted up into a steep incline. It took a few moments for him to recover and by the time he had, the four Scottish vehicles were tailing them, single file. The jeeps took a more relaxed pace up the mountain, relishing in their more powerful engines and superior tires, but Rory managed to keep a safe distance ahead of them.

Tiny independent shops flashed past as they wound their way up the hill, only to meet more roadblocks, a mixture of jeeps and bikes. Rory was forced left again, and again, until they faced the mighty Edinburgh castle itself. All vehicles that had herded them up here closed in, and Rory was forced to press on to the wide expanse of stone that lay before the castle. As they reached it, their pursuers spilled out from the approach, forming a wider line that shattered any hope of doubling back.

Rory turned the car around to face them and stopped. Emilia desperately looked around for an exit. But there was none.

Soldiers filed out of their vehicles, weapons raised, forming a regimental line in front of them. Like a firing squad.

Callum and Rory were silent. Emilia mustered enough strength to whisper.

"I'm sorry."

That's when the woman appeared.

19

Emilia hadn't encountered her since the Harwich Massacre, and time had not been kind to her. Nevertheless, there was no mistaking the police officer who ordered her troops to open fire.

"End of the line, witch," Hawthorne called. "Step out of the car, move away from your accomplices and come with us."

Emilia, Rory and Callum remained silent, fearful eyes locked on the captain.

"Harris," she barked. "Don't make me come over there. Step out of the vehicle and walk slowly over here."

Emilia wound the passenger window down slowly, slightly. The glass wasn't bulletproof but she still didn't want to give the soldiers, all nervously clutching assault rifles, a clear shot.

"What about my friends?" she called, trying to sound brave, in control. Fear betrayed her, broke her words into a squeak.

"We'll deal with them later," the captain sneered.

Rory's grip on the steering wheel tightened, but Emilia couldn't tell if it was from anxiety or defiance. He looked around for a gap in the line of black jeeps and motorbikes facing them, but there was none.

Callum gripped her shoulder. "Can't you do something? You've been crashing these vehicles left, right and centre."

"I...They..." Emilia reached out with her powers but struggled to see what good they would do. "There are too many of them."

She reached for the door handle, but yet again Rory's hand grasped her wrist. "Don't. The moment you're out of the car, they'll..."

He didn't need to finish. None of them could take their eyes off the array of guns.

The captain signaled to soldiers either side of her.

"Advance," she called, and a wall of armoured men and women slowly stepped towards the car.

Instinct compelled Rory to hurriedly put the car in reverse and they lurched backwards. The movement caught the soldiers by surprise, but none fired. Not until the captain yelled: "Tyres."

It was impossible to know which sound came first. The popping of rubber, the hissing of air and the audial barrage of bullets all combined so quickly, Emilia struggled to follow the frightful symphony that enveloped them. But as the car sank, so did both the shoulders of her companions and her hopes of escape.

And yet they remained in the car.

Hawthorne opened her mouth to unleash another command, but a taller man in a smart uniform - different to that of the captain - pushed his way through the soldiers and stared her down.

"What the hell do you think you're playing at?" he yelled. "Under no circumstances are you allowed to open fire on Scottish citizens."

"That's the escaped witch," the captain protested.

"Aye, and with her," the man gestured towards the car, "are two of my citizens and you are not to take another shot at them."

"They're aiding and abetting -" the captain began.

Emilia did not hear the rest of the captain's excuse. Instead, without turning to either Rory or Callum, she gripped the door handle and reached out for the frame of the car with her magic. Quickly gaining a firm grasp, she whispered to her two friends: "When I say the word, get out of the car as quick as you can and get behind it."

"What...?"

"Just do it, Callum," Rory hissed.

She sensed them grab their own door handles, none of them taking their eyes off the arguing officers. No time to waste.

"Now."

Emilia threw her door open and hurled herself out of the car, scurrying behind the boot. Callum was just ahead of her, stumbling slightly, and she heard Rory scrambling on the other side. As soon as she and Callum were clear, she wrenched the car around with her mind, turning it horizontally so it stood between them and the soldiers. The three of them crouched behind, slamming any open doors shut.

The captain roared in frustration. "Advance."

"Wait," the Scottish officer called. "Hold your fire. I repeat, hold your fire."

"You are interfering with an AMSF operation."

"And you are violating both the terms of our agreement and Scottish law. Hold your bloody fire."

"Advance," the captain yelled again. "But hold fire until my command."

Heavy footsteps clattered towards them along the stone. Rory and Callum looked expectantly at Emilia, and her eyes darted around for a solution. All that lay before them was more of the stone expanse, a short wall, a sharp drop, and the rest of Edinburgh sprawling away from the hill.

"Towards the wall," she said. "And stay low."

The two men lifted themselves up slightly, still ducking below the window line of the car, and crept forward. Rory grunted and groaned, suffering the pains of a position not meant for a man his age, but Callum cut across her to help him. The couple took each other's hands, and Emilia was once again reminded of the happy lives she had ruined with nothing more than her presence.

She crept forward too, also crouched, using her ability to pull the car along with them. The tyres scraped along the stone, the metal frame creaking as it moved in such an unorthodox manner, and the soldiers' footsteps momentarily stopped.

"Captain?" one asked.

"Keep after them, but hold your fire and keep a safe distance," Hawthorne responded.

They reached the wall and Emilia let go of the car, the vehicle creaking in relief. Rory squeezed Callum's hand, who hissed: "Great, now what?"

"I... I don't know..."

"Advance," the captain called. "Get around them."

Emilia collapsed against the car, every fibre of her being exhausted. She looked apologetically at Rory and Callum, tears welling in her eyes. Rory struggled to look reassuring, but it was Callum's face that surprised her. There was no anger there, no blame, no judgement. Just sympathy, and sadness.

The soldiers footsteps' grew louder as they approached, and Emilia could sense the armoured and armed men moving out and around the car. The line of them curled around the vehicle until men in black started to appear either side of them, guns trained firmly on the Wandless fugitive.

"We've got her, Captain," the one to her left shouted, a man behind him reaching for handcuffs attached to his belt.

There was a sudden rush of movement to her right and she realised Rory had stood up. She looked up to see him, arms aloft in surrender, shouting over the car roof towards the officers.

"Wait," he called. "Colonel, hear us out. Take us in and let her tell her side of the story."

"I'm afraid I can't do that, sir," the Colonel replied. "We have an agreement with the English."

"Which you said yourself she's breached. If you could just hear why..."

The soldier nearest to Rory raised his rifle and slammed it into his back. Rory's anguished yell snapped Emilia out of her despair and she looked up to see him crumple. Callum stood and barged between the soldier and his husband.

"Leave him alone."

"Get out of my way," the soldier spat, grabbing Callum by the shoulder and throwing him to the side.

Callum spluttered as he stumbled against the wall - then screamed as he tumbled over it.

20

Rory lurched towards the wall, shrieking his husband's name. The soldier trained his gun back on Emilia and barked something, but his words failed to penetrate as she threw all of her concentration after Callum.

He had already fallen several feet and he was only getting faster. She grasped for him with mental, mystical hands but he thrashed as he fell and she knew she was going to lose him. Then she connected and he hung in midair, his momentum arrested. Emilia was vaguely aware of Rory sobbing with gratitude. The soldier tried to walk past Rory to get to her, but the thunderous voice of the Scottish colonel stopped him in his tracks. Emilia slowly started to lift Callum towards them, but she could feel her limit approaching. Every mental muscle she possessed was on fire.

"Stand down. Hawthorne, have your men stand down."

"Soldier, arrest the Carrier."

"You will do no such thing," the colonel barked. "This is now a Scottish army operation. You just murdered a member of the Democratic Republic of Scotland. All AMSF troops are to lay down their weapons. Hawthorne, that includes you."

Raising Callum took almost everything Emilia had, but

she managed to retain some awareness of what was happening around her. Some of the soldiers around the car had already lowered their rifles, though none placed them on the ground. The soldier who knocked Callum over the edge stepped back, confused but holding on to his gun.

"Colonel, you have no right..." Hawthorne scowled in the distance.

"No, Captain, you have no right. Infantry, escort all AMSF troops back to command. Take those two into custody, but do not harm them."

Chaos erupted around them. Emilia wasn't sure who started it, still focusing on Callum, but as one Scottish soldier stepped forward to grab one of the AMSF, his English counterpart retaliated. Fists flew, guns were swung, helmets thudded and bones cracked. It was a sickening sound, drowned out by the rumbling in her ears as the effort to pull Callum back up sent blood rushing to her head.

At the very edge of her senses, she was aware of Hawthorne elbowing the colonel in the stomach and rushing towards the car. Rory's eyes were still locked on his husband, as if his intense glare would aid his ascent. For a moment, Emilia could see beyond Callum to the empty half-square of crooked buildings below and in a desperate flash, she saw the answer.

She reached out for Rory's hand. The touch of her hand caused him to look her way, confusion fighting through the distress. She hoped her own expression said, "Trust me," but there was no time to be sure. She pulled him to his feet and jumped forward.

The older man screamed, worse than he did when he saw Callum go over the edge. Hawthorne screamed as she watched them disappear from view. Callum screamed as he descended once more. Emilia's body screamed as she tried to slow the three of them as they fell.

She somehow managed to bring Rory and herself in line with Callum, but there was no time for relief as the rooftops below them rapidly approached. With both men beside her, Emilia collectively wrapped her power around them and concentrated on slowing down. All sound was drowned out by her heartbeat, pumping against her ear drums. She closed her eyes, but could still see, ignorant of what was above and all too aware of what rose up from below. They were no longer gaining speed, but neither were they slowing enough to land safely.

Emilia pushed away from the cliff face behind them, and they moved out from over the rooftops to above the pavement, buying a few more seconds. Every muscle, both physical and mental, ached. She could no longer feel any of her extremities, just her struggling mind and the two men she had connected to. She spluttered in relief as the ground's ascent began to slow and bunched her face up even tighter as she pushed away from it, an invisible barrier to cushion their fall.

They were just moments away from smacking into the pavement, but Emilia believed they had slowed enough to avoid breaking bones. She braced herself for impact, felt Rory and Callum tense up either side of her.

But she didn't feel solid ground. She felt nothing. Everything went black.

Hawthorne glared down at the three motionless forms on the ground far, far below. Anger swelled within her, bubbling up through her torso, unleashed as a guttural roar. The Carrier and her companions did not respond, did not move.

Then one of the men flinched, moved up onto his knees, tried to stand.

She reached for the pistol on her belt, but thick-gloved hands gripped her arms and pulled her away from the edge. The men and witch disappeared from view.

"No," she wailed. "What are you doing?"

She struggled, but whoever held her was too strong. She looked either side to see two Scottish soldiers wrestling her away from the wall, around the abandoned car and across the square.

The fight was over; her men either lying dead on the floor or kneeling down, hands on their heads. Scottish infantry filled the courtyard before the castle, at least two guns trained on every member of the AMSF - including Hawthorne.

The colonel stood at the centre of this restored order, his stance rigid. As Hawthorne was dragged nearer, he reached over to another of his infantry and took their handcuffs, readying them for the captain.

"Captain Hawthorne," he said, failing to disguise satisfaction as he walked around behind her to bind her wrists together. "Despite several warnings, you and your troops are guilty of multiple violations of the temporary alliance between our nations. You have endangered Scottish citizens, disturbed the peace, damaged property and even attempted murder."

"He's not dead..."

"Sadly," Reid continued, "you are still subject to English laws so there will be no punishment for you here. But you will all be taken to the border and sent back to where you came from. You will not be permitted to re-enter Scotland."

"But the Carrier -" she began as he paused for breath, now back in front of her.

"Will be dealt with by Scottish authorities. We will continue to search the area, apprehend her, and deal with her as we see fit. If we decide to send her back to England, we will contact the AMSF but it will be on the understanding that you are not in any way involved in that process."

"You can't do this," Hawthorne spat.

Colonel Reid merely nodded, prompting the two men who held her to drag her across the stones towards an awaiting Jeep. That was proof enough that he could.

21

Feeling returned. Softness. Then pain. Implausible amounts of pain, more than she had ever felt before. Every muscle was numb from some previous exertion but her pounding head blocked the memory of it. Every twitch and subtle movement as she writhed around in the comfort of... wherever she was... sent a fresh surge of hot pain through her body. Emilia moaned.

The noise attracted someone's attention. A gentle voice with a strange yet somehow familiar accent called to her, but her ears took a few moments to tune into their words, her brain struggling to process them.

"...you okay?" the man said.

"Where am I?"

"Castle Cocktails. The owner's private residence upstairs. They owed Callum a favour and agreed to let us rest up here."

The name triggered synapses in her mind, firing up to the point where it almost overpowered the agony. Almost.

Emilia reached out for her baby and instantly sensed their presence. Asleep, tranquil, and blissfully unaware of the pain their mother suffered. That was even more comforting than Rory's reassuring voice.

"Is Callum okay?" she asked, opening her eyes and

trying to sit up. "Are you?"

"We're both fine. Stay in bed. We can stay here for a few more hours."

"Wait, where's here? What's Castle Cocktails? I mean, I guess it's a cocktail bar, but how close are we to the castle?"

Rory chuckled. "Right underneath it. It's actually one of the rooftops Callum would have hit if you hadn't saved him. Saved both of us. It's really helped change his tune." He shuffled to get more comfortable. "Callum was the first one to recover from the fall. I did a few seconds later, and Callum was already trying to lift you up. You were completely out of it, so I helped him. We looked around and he recognised this place, so we dragged you inside."

"What about the soldiers?"

"Sounds like there was some sort of ruckus still going on up there when we brought you in," he said. "A bunch of them drove past here, some stopped and started knocking on doors for information about where we'd gone, but no-one saw us - there was no-one around because the Army cleared out the city centre once we were herded here. Just a few business owners stayed, but everyone seems to have kept their heads down. By the time the Army worked their way from door to door, we'd all managed to hide upstairs. They didn't search too thoroughly - it took them so long to get down here, I think they assumed we'd be miles away."

"What about that captain?" Emilia asked, shuddering at the thought of her harsh face.

"Haven't seen her. Matter of fact, haven't seen any of your English witchhunters. It's all been Scottish army."

Emilia sighed with relief, her whole body relaxing, sinking deeper into the safety of the mattress.

"So what's the plan?" she asked the ceiling. Rory answered.

"We're going to hide out here until nightfall - it's about

four o'clock in the afternoon. Once we're sure the coast is clear, we'll make our way on foot. We're not far from where you're heading, and it'll be too dark for people to really recognise you - and that's if anyone even ventures out into the city tonight. I imagine a lot of people will be staying in, just to be safe."

She chuckled. The sound surprised her. Already the pain was becoming more bearable, and she felt both her physical and magical strength returning. She reached out with her power and sensed Callum lying on a sofa in the next room, and one other person - presumably the owner - busying themselves downstairs - presumably in the bar.

Reaching out further, there were only a handful of people in the various buildings around the half-square below the castle. There were no military vehicles, no soldiers. All was quiet.

Relief washed over her, and a strange sensation built up within. Emilia endeavoured to identify it, trying to recall the last time she felt the same way. It had been before her escape, probably before her arrest all those years ago.

It was hope.

22

The air was cold as they stepped out into the street, a stark contrast from the warmth of the bed Emilia had woken up in. The bar owner had advised that they look inconspicuous, act as if they belong in order to avoid drawing attention, but none of them could resist a furtive look around to see if anyone was waiting. There was no-one around.

The castle loomed above them, illuminated by dozens of lights around its perimeter, a beacon of the past reminding the city of its history. As Emilia gazed up, she remembered a previous visit, the fascination she'd had with the ancient building, but now that memory was tainted with the events of the past day. Even a glimpse of the wall where Callum had tumbled over evoked the fear she felt in that moment.

That fear crept back in, the darkness striving to penetrate the radiance of the street lights, which threatened to produce new enemies - or worse, old ones. She pushed back at this feeling, casting it into the darkness itself. There was no sign of military activity, no sound of soldiers, no rumbling of engines. It was safe. For now.

Emilia followed Rory and Callum as they led her along the street, the three of them walking in silence. The city felt tense from the events of the day, but everything remained still. They only passed a few people as they walked, and all of them were focused solely on their own journey.

As they progressed through the dark city, she started to recognise places in the light of the street lamps. When they had hurtled through the centre of Edinburgh earlier, her eyes had mostly been closed, her concentration dedicated to fending off the troops that pursued them. Now that she was free to look around, it was strange to be back. Almost everything was familiar - the buildings, the road layout, the colour and texture palettes of the city - but a few changes, like new shops or cafés, were a constant reminder that time had moved on since her last visit. Returning to a place you once knew is a surreal but pleasant feeling, almost like discovering it for the first time all over again.

It wasn't long before they turned a corner and Emilia saw the block of apartments that they had been heading for, the building she'd had in her mind since she first decided to escape her Sanctuary. She had been picturing it regularly since first starting this journey, and yet was unprepared for the feeling of seeing the real thing. Her heart soared, her eyes watered and her legs began to shake.

"Rory, Callum," she said weakly. "Thank you."

She crossed the street without even looking. There were no cars, no movement, no sign of life in this part of the city. Her excitement grew as she reached the steps, and she practically skipped up them before stabbing the buzzer - she instantly remembered which one - with a quivering finger.

The buzz felt as if it echoed across the city, a grating and rude sound. But the voice that followed was the most angelic she had heard in years.

"Hello?"

"Lucy. It's me."

Another buzz and the door clicked.

"Quick," Lucy hissed through the speaker. "Get up here."

Rory and Callum maintained their silence as they stepped into the lobby with her. Their footsteps echoed across the tiles as they walked over to the lift, pressing the button and waiting the few, agonisingly long seconds it took to reach the bottom floor. Even with the mirrored walls, the lift was cramped and oppressive, but the lingering sound of Lucy's voice singing in Emilia's ears fended off any anxiety. As she gazed past her reflection, with its unkempt hair and sunken eyes, into the infinity afforded by two mirrors placed opposite one another, the Wandless could see futures she never imagined.

The lift emitted a chirpy 'ding' as they arrived on their required floor and the doors slowly slid apart. As soon as they were wide enough, Emilia stepped forward - but was thrown back by a sudden force grabbing hold of her. Her back slammed against the wall and she gasped. The tight grip on her instantly brought to mind the soldiers at the castle, and fear reared its ugly head once more. Was this an ambush? Did they know where she was heading? Was it a trap?

Yet there was an odd gentleness to this grasp, making it more of an embrace, and the head of her assailant was pressed firmly against her cheek. Instead of armour and muscle, Emilia felt soft clothes and the contours of a female body. And a familiar smell, a scent she had previously forgotten.

"Emilia," the woman cried, the exclamation muffled by the shoulder she had buried her face in.

"Lucy," she replied, and squeezed her back. Wrapping her arms around her half-sister was the epitome of relief. After all those years in the Sanctuary, Emila had forgotten the joy of human contact. She struggled to remember the last time she was this closely entwined with another human being. The obvious example sprang to mind, but it brought her predicament back to the fore. She pushed it away, longing to simply relish this moment.

Before she could savour another second, Lucy lurched back from her, grabbing her wrist and pulling her out of the lift. Rory and Callum followed, a little bewildered, as Emilia was dragged down the corridor and in through an open door, which, once her friends were also inside, was slammed shut behind them.

Emilia had stepped into the past. The apartment was just how she remembered it. There were some new photos and ornaments scattered around the room, plus a new sofa set, but the layout, the atmosphere and everything else was exactly the same. A home from home, the closest she'd had for a decade.

Lucy embraced her again. "Emilia, thank goodness you're okay. You shouldn't have come here, you really shouldn't, but I'm so glad you have." She looked up for a moment. "Who are these men?"

Emilia blinked at her for a moment, not understanding, then realised. The fugitive had been drinking in the sight of her sister's home since they had stepped in from the corridor. She shook off her confusion and stepped back to take each of her friends' arms.

"This is Rory, and his husband Callum. They're the most wonderful people I've met, they saved my life. They took me in last night, drove me here today and helped me escape the soldiers."

"Are you sure?" Lucy asked, eyes narrowing. "You sure no one followed you?"

"No. The streets are empty. And they wouldn't know to look for me here."

Lucy bit her lip. "Actually, they knew exactly where you were going. That's why there's so many soldiers in Edinburgh. This English woman, a captain, came here yesterday - she knew about us. She wanted me to signal them when you got here."

Fear trickled like ice down Emilia's spine. "We'll go. I'm so sorry, Lucy."

She turned to go but Lucy grabbed her wrist again. "No, wait. They've just said on the news that the English have been sent home. It's only our Army looking for you now, and they're widening their search beyond Edinburgh. We'll hide you here for the night and try to get you out of the city in the morning."

"Thank you, Lucy," Emilia said, tears forming once more.

Her sister smiled back, then blinked as she remembered they were not alone. She hugged each of Emilia's companions.

"Thank you so much for looking after her. I'm Lucy Anderson. It's a pleasure to meet you both."

Rory frowned, confused. "Anderson? I thought you were..."

"Half-sisters," Lucy said. "Our father met my mother while up here on business. It was only when she died that she told me where he was, and I found out I had a sister. We tried to keep in touch as much as we could, even visited each other when we could, but it became more and more difficult. And then..."

"Then I got arrested," Emilia finished.

Rory nodded in understanding. Lucy turned back to Emilia.

"I can't imagine what you've been through," she said, taking her hands. "You need to tell me everything, but first - is what they're saying true?"

Emilia tensed. The truth had been such a dark secret since the possibility first occurred to her. It was the source of her fear, the reason for her flight, the fact that had endangered both Rory and Callum's lives. And yet in this scenario, asked for by a loved one so cherished, the truth became the wonderful news it should always have been.

"Yes," she said, "It's true. You're going to be an aunt."

Lucy wept. They were tears of joy.

A few minutes later, they all sat on the sofas, Rory and Callum held each other close, as Emilia told Lucy all about her journey. Callum occasionally chipped in to clarify details or support her story, his tone softened, the judgment he once held gone. He described what happened after they fell from the castle, and thanked her again for saving him.

Her sister listened intently, resisting the urge to ask questions, until they were done. Then the conversation took its inevitable turn.

"Are you going to keep the baby?"

"Yes," Emilia replied instantly. In the silent parts of her flight, and even before she had found a way to cross the Sanctuary fence, she had thought on this long and hard. There could only be one answer. Nevertheless, Lucy's face was a picture of surprise and confusion.

"But what kind of life can you give your baby? You're a fugitive now."

Emilia looked away, unable to meet her sister's gaze. The hope she had felt outside receded, like a frightened woodland creature burrowing back into its home. She knew she had made the right decision, but as she attempted to look beyond tomorrow, she realised how rash that decision was.

"I... I don't know," she stammered, trying to sound more in control than she felt. "I haven't thought that far ahead. I just knew it was the only way to save the two of us."

Lucy squeezed her hand, and Emilia turned to face her. Her sister smiled kindly. "We'll work something out. I promise. I have some friends who may be able to help."

Callum raised his hand, a schoolboy gesture requesting permission to speak. He blushed as the two women turned to look at him.

"Sorry, but what do you mean by friends? Surely the fewer people who know about Emilia, the better."

"Equality For Witchkind," Lucy replied. "It's a group that fights for the rights of Scottish magic-users, calls for the lifting of some of the restrictions we have up here. We also help out the English group Free The Wandless where we can. There's rumours we've helped a few escape into Scotland over the years, but no one I know has confirmed it. Can't imagine E4W would ever admit it - it would destroy our reputation as a legitimate, democratic lobbying group."

"Are there many of you?"

Lucy nodded. "More than you might think. I know Scotland is more apathetic than England to the Wandless situation as a whole, but a lot of us still believe there's work to be done. They're no different to us - and we think we're starting to gain some influence. I heard today that there might even be a high-ranking Scottish Army officer on our side - a Colonel Reid. He came here last night with that dreadful English captain and kept her in check."

Rory frowned. "A colonel stepped in to stop the captain at the castle. He caused the diversion that let us get away."

"What did he look like?" Lucy grinned as Rory described him. "Sounds like him. I wonder if he's the one diverting troops away from the city centre. He must assume you were coming to me, like the captain did."

Emilia fought back a tear. The notion that there were

people out there actively fighting for her - not just her, but all those like her - fuelled that blossoming hope. Maybe, just maybe she could be safe up here.

“If there are groups like that down south,” Rory asked, “why on earth are Emilia’s people treated like this? Why are mothers...?” His voice trailed off.

"That's how it is down in England," Emilia said. "We aren't human. We're Wandless."

She heard her own words and wondered if she had reverted to accepting the barbaric way of life cultivated by her home nation. No. It wasn’t that she accepted it. More that she had distanced herself from it - literally. There was a border between her and the horrors she had escaped. Strange to think that the same border was a barrier to her just a day ago, another threat she had faced. Now it was a source of comfort, of protection.

"Do you mind if I ask...?" Lucy began, paused, then found the courage to finish. "Who's the father?"

Emilia’s face burned as it filled with colour and she looked down at the blanket. "He's not important," she said, instantly regretting her words.

"Not important? He's the father of your child. You're not the Virgin Mary. Who was he? Were you involved?"

"No, it wasn't like that. It's... It's complicated. He doesn't know I'm pregnant. I only found out from the doctor two days ago, and I escaped that night. I didn't think, I just ran. I had to protect the baby, protect myself, I..."

The lump that had formed in her throat choked her. Lucy stroked her blanket-covered leg.

"I'm sorry. I was just asking. You don't have to tell me."

"It's not that," Emilia croaked. "It's just... It was only a one-time thing. I don't know him that well. I mean, we'd been talking for a few weeks. He came around to my house one evening, so we could get to know each other a little better and - well, we both got carried away."

There was no way of explaining how the loneliness, the claustrophobia, the numbing dread of knowing you will spend the rest of your life trapped within a fenced off village drives you to seek whatever comfort you can find.

"Is he still at the Sanctuary?"

"I... No," Emilia sighed. "We think they found out about us - there's so much surveillance around the Sanctuary. He was transferred to another Sanctuary a week later. They do that sometimes if they suspect any of us are getting too close to one another. It's another way to prevent a potential uprising."

There was a moment of silence, and she couldn't help but wonder if the three of them were trying to imagine what a life without intimacy or even friendship might be like. She hoped they would never find out.

Lucy broke the dark and pensive moment. "I'll make some calls about a doctor in the morning. You can stay here as long as you like. I'm sure we'll be able to hide you if anyone comes searching, but I don't think they will. I know it will be difficult being cooped up in here for months but..."

"Not like I'm not used to it," Emilia sniggered. Humour now? It was incredible how quickly your perspective on the world could shift, especially in the company of such wonderful people. "Thank you, Lucy, but you really don't have to. If I can lie low for a while, then I'll..."

"You'll what?" Lucy raised an eyebrow. "Go where? Stay, you muppet. I've plenty of room, I can look after you, support you through the pregnancy and... I've missed you."

"I've missed you, too."

The sisters smiled at each other, remembering the great times they'd had on previous visits. Emilia's mind instantly flashed back to posing for photos in front of the castle all those years ago. The memory began to lift the taint left by the afternoon's experience.

"That's settled then," Lucy said.

"It is. But only until the baby is born. Then I need to move on."

"Why?" Lucy asked, looking hurt.

"Because they'll be dangerous," Emilia said. "That's one thing the AMSF has right - an infant witchkind is unable to control their power. We can't risk keeping them in a populated area - someone will find out. Didn't I hear that all witchkind births are registered up here? That you have special hospitals where they help mothers calm and control their babies' powers?"

"We do, but..."

"But I can't get into one of those, no. Of course not. But if we can find somewhere remote, somewhere away from people, I can raise them on my own."

"Emilia," Lucy said. "You can't. That will be so difficult."

"It's better than the alternative."

This time, Rory raised his hand. The two sisters looked at him, amused by his timidity.

"Actually," he said. "I have an alternative. Callum, dear, can I speak to you in private?"

23

"Where will you go?" the lieutenant asked her.

At first, Hawthorne ignored the question. It was perfectly obvious where she would go. And, equally, it was none of his business. She was a free citizen now - much as it pained her to admit it.

Her clothes were, oddly, much less comfortable than the tight-fitting uniform she had worn all those years. The fabric of her shirt felt softer, weaker than the one she had previously been issued, as evidenced by how she felt the evening breeze sift through the material, chilling her. Similarly, her shoes - lighter, more casual than her military boots - made her feel less sure of her footing. They were comfortable, sure, but now she had to deal with newfound concerns like stubbing her toes or people stepping on them. Hawthorne doubted she would ever get used to this.

She surveyed the scene around, a twilit Tweedmouth street with only a few moving cars and less than five pedestrians walking by. It was if the world was retreating in fear now she had been unleashed. That was perhaps the only good thing to come out of this: while she lacked authority now, they had inadvertently released her from the shackles that authority forced upon her. A grin spread across her face.

"Cap... Ms Hawthorne," the lieutenant said. "Maybe the General is right. This is an opportunity for you to do whatever you want, start afresh. Why not head south and see what the rest of England has to offer outside the Force? Find a home, rediscover yourself, or..."

"Shut up," she spat. The lieutenant fell silent, if only out of habit. "I will do what I please. There is no need to rediscover myself - I already know perfectly well who I am. I am the one who has never let a Wandless escape since the Sanctuaries were first built. I am the one who does not accept unfinished business. I am the one who..."

Hawthorne stopped herself. She did not need to justify herself, not to him. The lieutenant was one of them. Funny how it took just a few hours to accept that she no longer was. She turned to face him, saw the conflict on his face and felt an odd surge of compassion. Hoping it wouldn't last, she placed a firm hand on his shoulder.

"You're a promising officer, lieutenant," she said. "But never forget that you're England's front line of defence. The General and his lackeys judge everything on reports dumped on their desks by cowardly officers who prefer to have a keyboard to hand than a gun. They don't remember, know or care what we're actually dealing with, what the witchkind are truly capable of if they escape. You remember, you know, and you care. Oh, you have to follow orders - of course you do - but never let those orders get in the way of doing what must be done."

The lieutenant opened his mouth to speak, but only for a moment, unsure of what to say. Hawthorne simply saluted, and he saluted back. No other words were needed.

It was strange to think this was her last salute. She had always cherished them as a gesture of her position, her strength, her belonging. Just one day ago she would have reflexively, happily saluted any senior officer that passed her. Now she had an entirely different gesticulation in mind.

The journey to the border had been surprisingly quick after her humiliating arrest at Edinburgh Castle the day before. An embarrassing number of AMSF troops had been at the border to collect her - and just her. The lieutenant and the rest of her men had been left at the castle courtyard to await larger military transports that could take them back to England in bulk. But Hawthorne had been taken in Colonel Reid's personal car under armed guard, and shoved towards a line of men she had once commanded as they reached the border. The troops looked confused yet determined, and a little fearful - as if she were witchkind.

By midnight, she had been taken to an AMSF command centre in Tweedmouth, one that - ineffectively, she grumbled - protected the border and prevented Wandless from crossing, at least via the roads through the town. By morning, the General had arrived.

The inquiry had been long and infuriating. She had justified her actions time and again, but Colonel Reid had entered the room to sully the affair with his warped and naive version of the truth. What did any of that matter when there was a Carrier on the loose?

She had implored the General to end this farce and send her back north with more reinforcements, perhaps even a few of the tanks the AMSF had stationed in Tweedmouth. He had responded by calling another captain into the proceeding to list off her previous violations of proper investigative protocols. The General had insisted the incident at Edinburgh Castle was the straw that broke the camel's back. She said the camel was too weak to do what it took to keep the Wandless under control, and deserved to be crippled.

In retrospect, it was almost certainly this outburst that had sealed her fate. The General had stripped her of her rank, her uniform, her very position in the AMSF. She was forbidden from entering Scotland, from going anywhere within a five-mile radius of a Sanctuary or any other AMSF facility. She was a civilian, a nothing, adherent to the law, and she had better get used to it. One infraction, no matter how minor, and the consequences would be severe.

Hawthorne snorted as she recalled the General's threat. A low rumble to her left indicated the taxi she had ordered was approaching, and she waved to the driver.

"They'll never let you across the border," the lieutenant said.

The taxi pulled up and she opened the door. Just before she lowered herself into the seat, she shot the lieutenant a knowing look.

"They didn't let her cross either," she said, "but she found a way."

The taxi drove away. Ms Hawthorne never looked back.

24

Callum rolled his eyes as he descended the stairs. His husband still had his face pressed against the narrow, latticed window to the left of the cottage door. He could even see the fog created by Rory's warm breath on the cold glass, the man squinting into the darkness. A child hoping for a glimpse of Father Christmas would have grown bored by now. Callum cleared his throat.

"Still no sign of them, dear," Rory replied.

"Well, obviously. If there was, you might finally have torn yourself away from that bloody window."

He strolled towards the kitchen, pulling Rory by the shoulder as he did so. His husband shrugged off his grasp and maintained his vigil. Callum chuckled and stepped down through the archway. He filled the kettle and turned it on, then leaned against the kitchen units, watching Rory as he tilted his head to get a better view of their empty driveway.

"You think they're okay?" he called.

Callum sighed. "They're fine, Rory. Of course they're fine."

"It's just... We haven't heard from them in hours."

"One, dear," Callum said. "It's been one hour. Coming up on an hour and a half. And I imagine they're a little too busy to call or message. Lucy will be driving, and Heather will be..."

"Is that them?"

There was a dull thud as Rory leaned forward too quickly, bumping his head against the glass. A light flashed past the windows, another car on another journey.

Rory turned to face his husband, rubbing his forehead.

"Serves you right," Callum said. "Tea?"

"Please."

Callum watched Rory finally walk away from the window and slump into an armchair, before turning to prepare the drinks. As the boiled water cascaded into the cups, his memories of the past few months flashed before his eyes. Mostly, it was moments he and Rory had shared when the two ladies had left or spent the day elsewhere. It wasn't that he resented the times when they had all been together - far from it. He was surprised at how fond he had become of his new family unit and in such a relatively short space of time. It was more that he knew he would miss the tranquility, and the privacy he and his husband had enjoyed. They would get that back, of course, but not for a few years at the least.

"What were you doing upstairs?" Rory asked as he carried the two cups into the living room.

"Just putting something away," he replied after a moment, but his husband had already picked up on the hesitation. He shot Callum a knowing look, tilting his head to peer over invisible glasses.

"You were checking her room again, weren't you?"

"No, I was just... Okay, fine. Just wanted to be absolutely sure everything is ready. They'll be here soon."

"Jeez, and you were judging me?" Rory chuckled. "You're just as bad. We went through everything just yesterday. With Heather."

"I know, but I just..."

Both their heads snapped towards the door as tyres crunched over gravel and the low rumble of an engine came into focus. The engine stopped, a metal clunk signified the opening of a door, and the peaceful night's silence was shattered by a penetrating yet precious sound.

A baby's cry.

Rory nearly fell face first as he ran to the door, Callum close behind him. He wrenched it open, enduring the rush of cold air, and they both watched as Lucy helped her passenger out from other side of the car. The baby's cry grew louder and nearer, despite how tightly they were bundled up in blankets and held to their mother's chest. The woman never took her eyes off the child, but even at this angle, Callum could see she was smiling.

She finally looked up as she reached the doorstep. Heather Anderson, formerly known as Emilia Harris, beamed.

"May we come in?"

Rory practically dragged her by the arm towards her preferred armchair as Callum stepped outside to help Lucy with the bags.

"How is she?" he asked. "And how's the little one?"

"They're both absolutely fine," Lucy smiled. "Emilia kept asking whether we should go back to my place. She's worried they'll both be a burden to you."

"She's still worried about that? We agreed to this months ago. Not sure what more we can do to reassure her."

"You know how she is."

Callum nodded, comically rolling his eyes for added effect. By the time they were both inside and the cottage door closed behind them, Emilia was already sitting, gazing in wonder at the wriggling baby in her arms. The warmth and soft crackling of the fire had calmed her somewhat, her once piercing cries now reduced to tired but soft moans.

Rory had perched on the arm of the chair and was smiling down at the girl, barely able to contain himself.

"What's her name?"

"Lottie," Emilia sighed contentedly, stroking her daughter's wispy black hair. "It means woman with freedom."

Callum smirked as he watched his husband unleash a stream of happy tears, then subtly tried to wipe away the ones forming around his own eyes.

"Welcome home, Lottie," Rory said. "I'm your Uncle Rory. It's so very nice to meet you."

Lucy and Callum moved closer, and gazed down at the newborn girl, who watched them intently. The sight of the four faces above her were intriguing, and the moans slowly died away as Lottie stared back up at the new family that gathered around her.

THANK YOU

for taking the time to read Wandless.

I hope you enjoyed it. If so, I would be most grateful if you left a review on Amazon and/or Goodreads. If you think someone else might enjoy this book, let them know about it too.

DON'T FORGET

For regular updates on future books, including more Wandless stories, please subscribe to my mailing list

subscribe.jamesbatchelor.me

ACKNOWLEDGEMENTS

First of all, a huge thank you to my family and friends who have supported me - especially my wife, Penny, who has always encouraged me to make time for writing, to press on to the end of each project (and who has put up with me frequently using her for brainstorming sessions as I tried to navigate the story).

Thanks also go to my wonderful friend Layla of Parry-Hide Photography, for both the excellent cover design and the photoshoot at the heart of it, and to my sister-in-law Beth, for agreeing to model (not that you took much convincing).

I really appreciate the time and effort spent by Jay Mayo, Gemma Rule, Dominic Sacco, Alex Shaw, Sharon Shaw, Haydn Taylor and my sister Sarah (plus anyone I've forgotten, but I'm fairly confident that's all of you), who read the early versions of this book and helped me to refine it.

And lastly, let me express my gratitude again to you, dear reader. Without you, I'm just delving into my own worlds alone. I hope you'll join me for another adventure in the future.

ABOUT THE AUTHOR

James Batchelor is a journalist and your next favourite not-yet-bestselling author. He has written for leading B2B publications in the video games industry, and edited and contributed to charity anthologies by the Chelmsford writing group Writebulb.

James lives in Essex with his wife and two suspiciously adorable children, where he is currently working on Big Bad Wolfe, the first entry in the Death & Fairy Dust fantasy thriller series.

He refuses to admit he prefers e-books to paperback.

www.jamesbatchelor.me
facebook.com/jamesbatchelorauthor
twitter: @James_Batchelor

Printed in Great Britain
by Amazon